A KINGDOM RULED BY FEAR

A Novel By

Mark J. Brown

Contents:

Dramatis Personae 5

Chapter 1 7
Chapter 2 10
Chapter 3 17
Chapter 4 22
Chapter 5 27
Chapter 6 31
Chapter 7 34
Chapter 8 40
Chapter 9 47
Chapter 10 52
Chapter 11 56
Chapter 12 64
Chapter 13 71
Chapter 14 78
Chapter 15 84
Chapter 16 89
Chapter 17 95
Chapter 18 101
Chapter 19 108
Chapter 20 114
Chapter 21 120
Chapter 22 127
Chapter 23 134
Chapter 24 139
Chapter 25 147

Dramatis Personae:

Sorlian Royal Family and Entourage:
- King Cassien, King of Sorl
- Queen Alsarra, his wife
- Lady Jessa, his niece and ward
- Commander Ostion, commander of the palace guard
- Deel, poet, playwright and King Cassien's fool

Sorlian Segrata:
- Commissar Fadrinar, head of the Segrata
- Keph, cook in the palace kitchens
- Jerl, Keph's younger brother and member of the palace guard
- Nard, personal valet to King Cassien

Bronze Keep:
- Baron Gadric, Master of Bronze Keep
- Prince Borden, his eldest son
- Prince Locan, his second son
- Prince Talan, son of Prince Borden
- Drogan, soldier in the Bronze Keep army

Other:
- Nadia, courtesan
- Vict Reiden, palace cook and Segrata prisoner
- Crippled veteran
- Alster, carpenter and Segrata prisoner

Chapter 1.

Blood spattered onto the floor yet again, accompanied this time by the crunch of shattering bone. Keph moved away and held his hand up to the candlelight, watching the crimson stain on his fist shimmer in the amber gleam. A small trickle of blood ran down his finger and dripped onto the candle, causing a horrible, serpentine hiss to penetrate the silence of the dark chamber.

The room was small, cold, and dark. There was no window, no carpet, no lamp. The floor, walls and ceiling were all made from the same heavy, dull grey stone. A solitary candle lit the centre of the chamber with an orange glow. Beyond that single circle of light, the edges of the room receded into a thick shadow until they disappeared entirely from sight. The air was heavy with the sweat and the blood and the fear of decades of prisoners, the most recent of whom knelt in the light of the dying candle, hands manacled to the floor, nose broken and bleeding, head hung low.

Keph moved back to the prisoner and raised the man's head with his bloody hand, making sure his own face was concealed in the darkness of his hood. A gaunt, bearded, wretched face stared back at him, eyes dark and tired, yet resolutely defiant.

'You're a broken man, Alster,' Keph said. 'Look at you: you've had enough of all this, haven't you? All the pain, all the blood, all the fear. You know exactly how to make it stop. You have only to say a few words and all this will be over. You will be a free man.'

'A free man,' Alster spat. 'I can't remember the last time I was one of those.'

Keph let his prisoner's head drop again, and then slammed his boot into Alster's already broken nose. More blood cascaded as Alster's head whipped backwards, an anguished cry echoing off the hidden walls as the candlelight revealed for the first time the true extent of the scarlet mess that had once been his nose. He struggled against the chains that prevented him using his hands and cursed as he spat a clot of blood at Keph's feet.

'I'm going to ask you again,' Keph said quietly. 'I want the truth, otherwise I'll do worse than break your nose. Where is the manuscript?'

'I don't know anything about a manuscript.'

'Lies! You have had four known dissidents visiting your house three times a week. One of those is already in our custody and has revealed that the five of you were working on a subversive and insurrectionary manuscript. We brought another in this morning, who told us after three hours of intensive interrogation that you were the man responsible. So, I ask you again, where is the manuscript?'

'I'm not going to tell you anything.'

'Are you sure about that?'

The hard look in Alster's eyes was all the reply Keph needed. He moved slowly to the candle and snuffed it out with his fingers, plunging the room into a cold, close darkness. He reached across to his hip and grasped the hilt of the blade that hung there, drawing it from its sheath with a long, endless ring. Then he stood in silence, listening to Alster's ragged, fearful breathing.

He counted the seconds in his head with practised perfection.

Fifty-seven . . . Fifty-eight . . . Fifty-nine . . . Sixty.

He began to walk slowly, precisely, letting every step he took echo in the emptiness, trailing the sword on the stone floor with an infinite, grating drone until he stood behind Alster. It was a spot in which he had stood countless times before. From here he knew exactly where the door was, where the candle was, and where his prisoner was. Again he stopped and stood in silence as Alster's breathing became more rapid, more frantic, more desperate as he tried in vain to keep it under control.

Twenty-eight . . . Twenty-nine . . . Thirty.

Keph raised the blade, placing the keen edge lightly against the back of Alster's neck, before drawing it slowly backwards and forwards in a gentle sawing motion. He felt a slight change in pressure as the blade bit into the soft skin. He felt his prisoner pull away and press himself towards the floor. He knelt down and replaced the blade on Alster's neck, before whispering,

'Where is the manuscript?'

Alster didn't reply.

'Do you value your life?' Keph continued. 'Do you value your existence? Think of all those nice things you have in this world: your home, your livelihood, your family. You won't leave all of those behind just to protect a bunch of papers. Do you hate your family that much? Do you really hate them so much that you would be willing to die and leave them to grieve for you? How many children do you have, Alster? Five? They need a father to grow up with, and you would deny them that because you can't let go of your pursuit for a new government? That is selfish and cruel.'

He slid the blade back and forth again, biting deeper into Alster's neck, then removed it. He did not have to be able to see his prisoner to know that the blood would already be dribbling down the back of his neck, sharp, heavy and warm.

'Where is the manuscript?'

'What happens if I tell you? What happens to me? Is it an execution or a prison sentence?'

He was starting to break. Keph could hear it in his voice. Just a little more encouragement was required.

'If you tell me now, you walk free. But you will still be under Segrata observation. We can't risk you getting subversive ideas again, can we?'

He slammed the pommel of the sword into Alster's shoulder. The sharp snap of bone ricocheted off the unseen walls. So did Alster's scream.

'Either I break the other one and you get a prison sentence, or you tell me now and walk free. Where is the manuscript?'

'There's a trapdoor in the kitchen floor!' Alster's voice was as cracked and broken now as the rest of him, tears of both pain and frustration choking his throat. 'Everything's under there: the papers, the manuscript, everything. It's all there, now let me go! Let me go, please.'

Keph stood up and sheathed the sword, before moving back to the candle and relighting it. At the sudden return of light, Alster blinked and lowered his eyes, wrenching his hands against the manacles. Once adjusted again, he looked back up at Keph. Where before his eyes had been stoically resolute, now they were merely empty and tired. The blood around what was left of his nose was starting to harden and flake off. His shoulder was offset now, at a crude angle, and a steady stream of blood ran from the back of his neck, down inside his ragged shirt.

It was a fate Keph had inflicted upon countless people.

'You're not the first man to look like this,' he remarked, removing the key to the manacles from his pocket and starting towards Alster. He knelt down again and clicked the key into the lock. 'And you won't be the last either.'

Chapter 2.

The human race is a flawed race. Among its people there are many who are noble and generous, and yet there are others, more selfish and arrogant, who believe they are so superior to everything and everyone around them that nothing matters except themselves and their aims. A casual observer would remark on how few people like this they see in the world, and they would endeavour to see the world in a good light. What the casual observer would not see is that the humans who have these flawed qualities, these delusions of their own self-importance, are the ones who are born into the noble families: the kings, the queens, the lords, the ladies and all the rest of the aristocracy.

They not only have inherent power and authority, but they know how to wield it to further their own aims at the expense of their people. On the outside these rulers and so-called *nobles* are proud and demeaning and arrogant. But on the inside, they're scared.

Fear governs rulers. And, by extent, that same fear governs entire kingdoms.

They are scared because they have never known what life is like without the power, wealth and authority that their station provides. They have never had to live without a comfortable bed and a staff of servants to wait on them, without full meals every day and entertainment every evening to satisfy their needs.

They don't want to lose what they have because they fear what life will be like once it's gone.

This is the same problem faced by King Cassien of Sorl.

From birth he had been raised as a warrior more than a diplomat. He was a warlord more than a king. And, like all warlords, he sought to settle a dispute with a sword rather than with words. He ruled through fear.

He covered his own fear by making others fear him.

Fear does, indeed, govern kingdoms.

King Cassien was a strong warrior – tall, broad and bearded – and was considered one of the masters of the arts of duelling and warfare. He felt no need for words and diplomacy whilst there was still room to swing a sword, so when his subjects complained or expressed dissatisfaction, no matter how small or trivial, he crushed them like insects. Had he been inclined to learn how to talk properly with his subjects, he could have settled matters equally amicably for both parties. But he didn't learn. He never did.

Instead of respecting his subjects, as any decent ruler should, his heart turned to stone, his fist turned to iron, and his head became filled with nothing but his own authority. He feared that any attack on him could dethrone him and leave him stranded in the gutter for rats to spit on, and he had no intention of letting that happen.

He governed his kingdom through fear. Pure, sheer fear.

And to instigate this fear he employed one of his father's most trusted advisers: Fadrinar. And Fadrinar put together the Segrata: agents of Cassien's regime used in order to root out dissent and rebellion and crush it without mercy.

Nobody knows how many died from the activities of the Segrata. Nobody kept a record.

Fadrinar, newly promoted to Commissar of the Segrata, was not a brutal man. But he had his goals and he achieved them. He was, more than anything else, a loyal man, and this, as far as Cassien was concerned, was all the Commissar of the Segrata needed to be. Unquestioned loyalty would ensure that when the time came to put fear even into Fadrinar's heart, he would do whatever he was ordered to, regardless of the consequences.

It was a technique Cassien used with many of his ministers.

Among the Segrata were people from all walks of life. Some were nobles in Cassien's court, spying on the other aristocrats in a game of sharp wits and political intrigues. Others were citizens out in the city – shopkeepers, bartenders, seamstresses with their ears to the ground and their eyes open for treachery. Some were slightly further afield, secreted in the armies of the other nobles or in the more rural villages, where rebellious rumours are spread without fear of authority.

Until the mysterious disappearances start.

And there were some among the palace staff, the menials at the butt end of Cassien's retinue. Among these was Keph, a servant in the palace kitchens, where among the clatter of pots and pans and the shouting of the head chef, undesirable conversations could easily take place.

Keph, like Fadrinar, was not brutal or ruthless. He just got on with his job. At first he had leaped at the idea of serving the king as an undercover agent, but the job was less glorious than he had first expected. There was killing, and shadowing people, arresting and torturing them to make sure that they would never again be a threat to the king and his people. But once a man was in the Segrata, he never left it. If he tried, he was killed.

He had seen it done before.

He was, Fadrinar kept telling him, one of the more efficient Segrata operatives. Among the palace servants there was a lot of discontent, and it took only one servant to say something they shouldn't in a voice loud enough for Keph to hear, and they were lucky to be seen again.

The servants knew the Segrata existed – indeed, neither the king nor the commissar made any effort to conceal the fact – but until the disappearances they never knew that one of their own number was an agent. Even then, they never knew it was Keph.

Only one person outside of official channels knew about Keph's affiliation to the Segrata. That person was Deel: poet, playwright and fool to the king. There was no telling how Deel found out about it, but he had managed it all the same, regardless of the multiple layers of secrecy and caution protecting the agents' identities. Not only was he a good friend to Keph, he was also just as good a friend to Jerl, Keph's younger brother. Jerl too had found himself part of the Segrata, though somewhat less enthusiastically than many of the other agents. And where Deel had followed his passion for literature and poetry, Keph had gone into cookery, and Jerl was in the palace guard, keeping tabs on certain soldiers, as well as on Commander Ostion himself, as part of his Segrata duties.

Deel had once described himself very aptly as a 'ruffled sort of owlish-looking fellow'. The tousled thatch of hair, the slight hunch and the thick neck did indeed make him look like an old owl. But the stark, mad sparkle in his dark eyes was more than a slight indication of his potential insanity. On most subjects Deel would have a large amount to say, but on the subject of his own psychological health he found himself having to be either gagged or left alone in a locked room before he finally stopped raving.

Being a close friend of Keph, he would come down to the kitchens after Cassien, his wife Alsarra and their niece and ward Jessa had all retired to their chambers for the evening in order to alleviate his inevitable boredom. Deel would talk and Keph would clean the place up, long after the rest of the servants, and even the head chef, were gone to bed.

It was on these occasions that Deel would throw around ideas for his next play or piece of poetry. Keph would listen and occasionally suggest, but most of the time he only half listened. After a while it became all too easy to shut Deel out completely.

'I had another idea earlier today,' Deel said. 'It came to me after hearing the dispute in court this morning. The one between the Barrock and the Valgar families. They absolutely detest one another. Now, I was thinking, what if their children were to get to know each other? Fall in love even? What then? What would the parents do? What would their friends do? What would they do?'

'Sounds a little light to me,' Keph remarked, piling some clean plates together. 'It doesn't sound as though much could go on except a load of disputes and arguments between the parents.'

'It would focus on the children, not the parents.' Deel began to pace, gesticulating furiously with his hands. 'Besides, it's a romance. The main part of it is the love, however forbidden.'

'People would lose interest if it just becomes a play full of professions of love. I know I would.'

'It needs some action then.' He stopped pacing. But the pause was only momentary. 'A duel, perhaps? A duel between the male lover and someone else. The man the girl is supposed to marry? A jealous suitor? A noble cousin of sorts? Yes, something exciting needs to happen.'

'Maybe they could climb a balcony while they're at it,' Keph said idly, wiping out a pan. 'That would get the audience going.'

'A balcony!' Deel's pacing grew more rapid, and he began to spin in circles, this way then that, his body as scatty as his brain. 'Yes! My word, Keph, you're full of ideas tonight. But a balcony scene would be wonderful, new, innovative. But how to stage it? Oh, never mind; that will come later. Perhaps not for the duel though – too dangerous for the actors to be leaping around on it.'

'For something else then,' said Keph, 'if you're so intent on using it.'

'Oh, I am. Most certainly. I shall have a balcony in my play if it's the last thing I do.'

There was a moment of silence. Keph wiped clean a second pan. Deel stopped suddenly as if frozen in place, absolutely motionless save for his eyes. As though of their own accord they began darting around the room, never stopping to rest on any one thing. But mere moments later he was pacing again.

'Perfect! The lovers! Imagine it!' He grabbed Keph suddenly by the shoulder. 'Imagine it: she's standing on the balcony, looking out over the moonlit garden or the city or something, pining for her lover. And then suddenly . . . there he is! Down below, looking up at her, he stands and professes his undying love for her. And then he climbs up to her and – '

'Deel,' Keph said quickly, removing his friend's hand from his shoulder. 'Spare me the gory details. If it's advice on romance you're looking for, don't come to me. Anything else is fine, but don't ask me whether I think something's romantic or not. You won't get a nice answer.'

'I'm sorry, Keph. But you see it's so invigorating for me, finding something new and exciting to do, to write about. Oh, and not only the balcony, but a romantic poem to go with it. The moon and the sun and the stars. It's romance, Keph, romance! The queen will love it!'

Ah yes, thought Keph. *The queen.*

Alsarra had been the daughter of Cassien's father's first minister. It was a marriage that had been arranged for her. It was widely known that she had always wanted and wished to marry for love, not because her father told her to, but not having fire or passion enough to fight against it, she was married off to Cassien. She had also made it publicly clear that she disliked Cassien and often resented her position. Not possessing the will to go against the dictates of her husband and society, she was often unhappy in public, and worse behind closed doors.

Deel, the clever writer that he was, knew that anything romantic would make Alsarra happy. Perhaps not Cassien so much, but he would allow it because he feared that if his queen was too unhappy for too long, she may at last rebel against him and have him overthrown.

Again, fear governed the king.

'Yes,' Keph admitted. 'I imagine she will.'

'I don't think I've had such a wonderful idea in years!' Deel continued. 'There's so much I could do with it, and so little space in my head to hold it all. I would stay and help you, but I just have to get all this down on paper. Wish me luck, Keph! It's going to be a long night.'

At a run, Deel left the kitchens, leaving Keph to wonder at his friend's enthusiasm.

'You'd stay and help me would you?' he said to thin air. 'When was the last time you did anything more than pass me a spoon?'

Considering how little experience he had with literature or art or acting, Keph considered himself well versed in it, solely due to his closeness with Deel. He had no skill as an actor or a playwright, but he could think and analyse and suggest, which is what Deel really needed. He was a scatty sort of person, his mind in all likelihood in three places at once, or even more. The ideas he could form, and he could envisage what would be said, how the characters would react, but he could never string anything together long enough to make it coherent.

Keph secretly wondered if all playwrights and poets were like that, or whether it was just Deel.

Without his presence a relaxing sort of stillness came over the kitchen. Keph quite enjoyed the rare silence.

One can only endure Deel for so long, he said to himself. *No wonder he isn't married.*

He closed the last cupboard and extinguished the last lamp, and left the kitchen, locking the door behind him. In the passage outside he encountered the night patrol. The pair of soldiers in their olive green uniforms greeted him with a 'Good evening,' and walked on. The palace guards knew from experience that they were not welcome in the kitchens, and were wary of treating the kitchen staff with anything less than respect; the head chef held a fearsome reputation with a carving knife.

At this time of night, it was only the night patrol and occasional servants in the palace corridors. The nobles of the palace would be in bed, either sleeping or plotting, and the staff would be preparing themselves for another busy day of work and toil. Deel, no doubt, would be scribbling away by candlelight in his small paper-strewn study near the royal quarters. Cassien and Alsarra liked to keep their fool close at hand.

Their niece and ward, however, was not even in the same wing of the palace. Where the royal apartments and banquet halls were located in the north wing, the Lady Jessa was, conveniently enough for both herself and the king, situated in the east wing, which housed the libraries and archives of the palace, along with the museum. Really it was only a room full of things the king wanted to be rid of. But *museum* sounded grander.

The south wing would be empty, apart from the few servants left to maintain it. It was the wing that would house the king's guests. Not receiving many guests, however, the wing was little used.

Of all the wings of the palace, the west wing would be the busiest at this time of night; it contained the headquarters of both the Segrata and the palace guard, along with the armouries, training rooms and workshops to help maintain the soldiers' equipment.

It therefore came as a surprise to Keph when, upon reaching his room in the north wing, Jerl was waiting for him.

Though four years younger than Keph, Jerl was taller, broader, and stronger. Much of it was due to his training as a soldier, but even before he had enlisted he had been the bigger of the two. Dark haired and dark eyed, Jerl was considered handsome by many of the female servants. It was something he had learned to ignore.

'Jerl!' Keph said, stopping short at the sight of his brother. 'What are you doing here?'

'Urgent message from Fadrinar,' Jerl replied. 'There's a meeting of all Segrata who work or live in the palace at eight o'clock tomorrow morning. Usual place.'

'And here was me hoping it was a late night social call,' said Keph. 'I haven't seen you for a week.'

'I know. Commander Ostion has had me doing extra duties. I think he wants to promote me soon.'

'I can't blame him. You're as capable a soldier as I know.'

'You don't know many soldiers then.'

'You're too humble sometimes, Jerl,' Keph remarked. 'One day you're going to have to have confidence in yourself and your abilities. Especially if you get promoted. Advice from an older brother.'

'Last time I took your advice we almost got lost.'

'True, but you have to remember that was back when you didn't know your right from your left.'

'Fair point.'

'Besides, things might be different this time.'

They stood in silence for a brief moment. Keph tapped the side of his foot idly on the wall. Then Jerl said, 'How was Deel this evening?'

'Almost unbearable. He's got some new idea for a play: rival families whose children fall in love against the wishes of their parents. He wants a balcony scene too. With poetry.'

Jerl nodded slowly.

'Do you think he's legal?' he asked suddenly.

'What?'

'Deel. Do you think it's legal to be as mad as he is?'

'I think mad might be the wrong word,' Keph said. 'Vigorous insanity combined with ravings of pure genius might be a little closer to the mark.'

'With words like that, you could become a poet too,' Jerl grinned.

'If that ever happens,' said Keph, 'please take me to the guillotine.'

'Depend on it.'

After another brief silence, Jerl continued, but significantly more sombre than before.

'That's a sad thought: you at the guillotine.'

'Then let's hope it never happens. Now then, little brother, why don't you go and tuck yourself up in your bed and think nice thoughts?'

'I would, but I'm on patrol on the wall in an hour. I'll leave you to yourself, and I'll see you in the morning at the meeting.'

'Until the morning then,' smiled Keph. 'If you're still awake after your patrol. Good night, Jerl.'

Jerl twitched his mouth into a smile and left, and Keph entered his quarters. It was a small room with a rickety but homely bed, a washstand and small mirror. Not even a window.

He turned out the lamp and lay down, wondering not only at Deel's overwhelming dynamism and Jerl's eternal modesty, but at the reason for Commissar Fadrinar calling such an urgent meeting.

Chapter 3.

The morning was cold and grey, the sun obscured by heavy clouds. Keph rose early and left his quarters, not wanting to wait around now that he was awake. He took a slightly circuitous route, using the time to stretch his legs a little, before arriving at the west wing at ten to eight.

The guard was changing, and the relative bustle of soldiers going on patrol and returning to the barracks was cover enough for Keph to wind his way through the corridors on the ground floor and reach a tower that remained locked on Fadrinar's orders. The wood of the door was old, but anyone who observed it closely enough would notice that although the door itself was showing signs of age and decay, the hinges and the lock were well used. Keph produced a small key from his pocket, slipped it into the lock and turned it. The door clicked open and he entered quickly, taking care to lock it behind him.

The stairs upwards were blocked by another, significantly heavier, door to which only Fadrinar held the key. The stairs downwards, however, were smooth and clean from years of regular use. Keph followed them down in a tight spiral until they levelled out into a short passageway that opened into a round chamber.

The chamber itself was not so out of the ordinary, but the table in the centre was; when King Cassien sanctioned the establishment of the Segrata, he had diverted a significant amount of money from the treasury to Fadrinar's own pocket so that the commissar could arrange whatever he needed with minimal difficulty. Fadrinar, however, had had other ideas. With shady contacts already established before he even made it into Cassien's court, Fadrinar was able to obtain what he needed through them at no charge. To avoid suspicion he spent the money on the table instead, having it built to satisfy his own taste for expensive furniture.

It was large, round and ornate, constructed from polished white wood and inlaid with carvings of lions and hawks. Fadrinar always said that he believed the Segrata were similar to both hawks and lions.

'We watch like hawks, and pounce like lions.'

Keph had always thought it was unoriginal. Deel had called it uninspired and lacking in *literary savvy*, whatever that was. Most people just called it corny.

Around the table were a number of basic wooden chairs, in which sat those Segrata members affiliated with the palace. Keph did not know all their names, but knew what they did. Besides himself and Jerl, there was one of the gardeners, the stable master, the valet to King Cassien himself, and a nobleman from the court, a lord of some sort. Keph had never bothered to learn his name.

It was not long before the commissar arrived. He was short and stout, with a receding hairline and sharp eyes. He wore the green vestments of a minister with the comfort and surety that only high society breeding can provide, and kept adjusting the scarlet sash trimmed with gold thread that marked him as Commissar of the Segrata.

'I'm glad to see you're all on time,' he said briskly. 'I apologise for any inconvenience, but this is an absolute necessity. I believe you all know about the dissident nobles in the northern marches of the kingdom. There have been developments. Serious developments with even more serious consequences. We knew already that they were discontent, but there has never been the justification to wage all out war.'

'Why in the Gods' names not?' demanded the noble. 'Crush them before they can rise up in full.'

'And how would you do that?' Jerl said. 'Once we begin to destroy them they will unite faster and stronger than they are now. We might not win, and even if we did we would lose a lot of men unnecessarily.'

'If it puts down these rebels, I would call it necessary.' The noble was on his feet now, hands planted firmly on the table.

'And how far would you go?' said Keph. 'Would you accept a surrender if it was offered, or would you slaughter every last one of them? Because if you slaughter them all, there will be nobody left to work the fields; those noble families own more than half of the kingdom's food sources between them. To wage a war on people who have not yet made a decisive move against the king would be ill advised.'

'Quite,' Fadrinar said. 'However, they may be about to make a decisive move. Up until now we believed that the dissidents were working in coalition. We believed they formed a council of sorts. But new intelligence has emerged. They follow the lead of Baron Gadric of Bronze Keep.'

'Gadric?' said the king's valet. 'He's no leader, surely.'

'I agree,' added the stable master. 'If they want to rebel, why not follow Duke Cardil? He has more campaigns under his belt than the rest of the dissidents put together.'

'Because,' said Fadrinar, 'it seems that they are open to talks. Gadric may not be much of a soldier, but rest assured he is among the shrewdest planners and negotiators in the kingdom. He has asked the king for an opportunity to talk about the disagreements on behalf of all the dissidents.'

'I doubt the king will accept though,' the gardener said. 'He won't, will he, commissar?'

'To the contrary. The king has welcomed the baron.'

'What in hell does he think he's doing?' Once again, the noble was on his feet. 'Gadric may not be aggressive, but Cardil is. Count Seldin, too, is a martial leader. Even if Gadric succeeds in winning the king over, Cardil and Seldin won't just let it all go! No, they will fight, regardless of what Gadric achieves.'

'And how do you know this so well?' Keph snapped. He remained seated, but stared hard into the noble's smouldering eyes. 'Are you in league with them . . . my lord? Or is it your arrogance that blinds you to reason?'

'You, boy, are but a servant! You do not have the right to challenge me like this.'

'He has every right,' Fadrinar said tersely. 'In this room you are all Segrata agents. Social position is irrelevant here. Around this table you are all equals. Treat each other like it.'

The noble subsided, slumping back into his seat. Fadrinar continued.

'The king may have agreed to hold talks with Gadric, but both are notoriously stubborn. I doubt they will reach an agreement on anything, but the king believes he has some offers that the baron would be foolish to refuse. More than that, he has not said. We must, however, be on our guard; Gadric may not be an aggressive leader, but both his second son and grandson have militant tendencies. It has also been reported that Gadric's retinue will consist of two thousand soldiers.'

'Two thousand?' said the stable master. 'Right here in the palace?'

'Correct.'

'What is the king thinking?'

'I would not question the king so readily, if I were you,' the valet said. 'I agree he may have slightly unorthodox methods, but he is more canny than he seems.'

'Jerl, how many in the palace guard?' said Keph.

'Twelve hundred. But many of us have only seen one or two battles. We may be drilled, but as a whole we have little collective experience. Most of Gadric's men are veterans, though. He's led three successful campaigns against the northern raiders in as many years.'

'That is exactly what I feared,' Fadrinar said. 'They will have more men as us, the majority of whom are better trained and more experienced. It is my belief that the king has overstretched himself this time. Anyone with a military brain can see the advantages Gadric has over us. If the king's talks fail, there will be almost nothing between Gadric and the throne of Sorl.'

'There'll be us though, won't there?' the gardener said.

'Yes, all seven of us,' said the stable master. 'What good can we do?'

'What good can we do?' said Keph. 'Have you forgotten what it is the Segrata is for? It's for the safety of the king and the kingdom. It would be a betrayal to ignore that. I for one will carry on regardless of the situation.'

'Well said.' From across the table, the valet gave Keph a smile of approval.

'Well said, indeed,' said Fadrinar. 'I already have a contingency or two in place. But we must be prepared to do whatever is necessary. If, or indeed when, the talks fail, you must all be ready to defend the king however you can. If there's an opportunity to kill the baron, or his sons, or his grandson, then take it. If you can sabotage them, then do. You must all be alert, and you must all be prepared. The baron is due to arrive in the palace this evening. He and the king will talk tomorrow. After that, I cannot say. But I must make absolutely clear that you make no move until Gadric has made his. I will not have one of my men starting a conflict which could have been avoided, because that man will not live out the week. You are all dismissed, except for you, Keph.'

Fadrinar's gaze shifted slowly to meet Keph's own. 'I have another interrogation for you.'

Keph waited as the rest of the agents filed out of the room, back into the palace to perform their daily duties. The prospect of another interrogation filled him with such a sense of depravity he wondered at his continuing to do it. And yet not to continue would be to refuse the Segrata, which would be the same as signing his own death warrant.

He had looked forward to serving the king, but he had never expected to become a torturer and executioner. And yet, when he was in there with the prisoner, he felt right at home. Causing pain, instigating fear . . . it was all too easy now.

Worryingly easy.

'I understand you dislike working with the prisoners,' Fadrinar said once the door had closed. 'I can't blame you; it's a dirty, gritty business, but our business all the same. I usually try to give my agents a significant enough break between interrogations to let them calm down a bit, remember they're still human. Your interrogation of Alster yesterday morning was quick and efficient, and I'm pleased with that. I would be happy to give you a bit of time off from the cells. But I'm afraid I need you and you alone for this one.'

'How so, sir?'

'The prisoner is a servant from the kitchens. Clearly, you will know him. That gives you an advantage – you know what he's like, what he responds to . . . how much punishment he can take.'

'And what do I need to get out of him?'

'He has been saying things which could be construed as subversive and rebellious against the king. We can't afford such dissent in the king's own servants with Baron Gadric on his way; it would be too much for us to handle all at once. I need you to make sure that this man will no longer say such subversive things. Make him give you his assurance he'll watch his tongue. Can you do that?'

It was clearly a threat more than a question, and a threat to which there was only one answer.

'I can, sir.'

'Thank you. I don't expect you to like this, but I'm glad you're willing to do it.'

There was, Keph knew from experience, a difference between being willing and being sensible.

Chapter 4.

Keph had lost count of the number of times he had donned that Segrata cloak, pulled it around his shoulders and clasped it in place about his neck. It was becoming more and more familiar to him now, reaching back and drawing the hood over his head. The worn cloth encroached into the edges of his vision, making the rest of the world seem that much more distant, as though he was watching everything he was doing through a window, isolated and alone.

The sword, too, had grown familiar, the leather-bound hilt and the keen, smooth blade almost a part of him now. It hung at his hip. It used to be heavy, cumbersome even, when he had first worn it, but it seemed to grow lighter with age; now it weighed so little upon him that he almost forgot he had it. It was becoming so natural, so right, to have it with him.

It was worrying.

He pulled the hood down a little more to ensure his face was hidden, then took the cell key from his pocket and clicked it into the lock. It turned without a sound and the door swung open, revealing the darkness beyond. Keph stepped through and closed the door behind him, locking it again and returning the key to his pocket.

The prisoner was stood in the middle of the room in the single circle of candlelight, each hand chained to an iron pole either side of him. His shirt and shoes had been removed, leaving him shivering in the cold.

Keph recognised the prisoner immediately. There was not one servant in the kitchen he did not recognise.

'Vict Reiden.' Keph's voice was loud in the darkness, and deeper than normal courtesy of the echo off the unseen walls. 'You have come to our attention as a potential dissident against the rule of His Majesty King Cassien. We have had reports from reliable agents that you have been at the centre of subversive conversations in the palace's kitchens and servant quarters. Don't bother to deny it, your word counts for nothing.'

'Then why am I here and not at the gallows?'

'Because what you have done does not warrant an execution, merely a warning and a guarantee that nothing of the kind will ever happen again.'

Keph pulled a match box from his pocket and moved along the edges of the room, lighting the candles set into brackets on the walls. Soon the whole room was lit, and the darkness receded. The true black hue of the stones was even more apparent in the bright light. Keph came to stand in front of Reiden, shifting his cloak so that the sword was visible at his hip. From beneath the hood he could see Reiden peering back at him, bright eyes sharp and piercing.

'You won't even show me your face,' said Reiden. 'You think that scares me? You think I'll be frightened by it?'

'No, I don't,' Keph said quietly. 'But it would be nice if you were. It might make my job less detestable.'

'Detestable? You people kill and terrorise out of hand! That's more than detestable.'

'Everything we do, however brutal, is necessary to ensure safety. Both your own, and the kingdom's. That means doing things we would rather not so that other people don't have to. Yes, it's detestable, but its also necessity. Would you like to cause pain and suffering every day of your life? No? Then let me do it so that you don't have to.'

'So what do you plan on doing with me if you're not going to execute me?'

'Ensure you never say anything subversive again.'

'And exactly what did I say that was subversive?'

'*Imagine what it would be like if I was king.*'

'That was a harmless speculat – '

Keph's fist cracked across his jaw.

'Harmless speculation? How about *People go funny if they're in power for too long?*'

'A passing remark. General observation.'

'Observation of whom?'

Keph's fist flew again, cracking into Reiden's jaw for a second time.

'Of Commander Ostion. People say he's losing his touch in his old age. They say he's not as good as he used to be.'

'Do they?'

A third crack across the jaw. This time something snapped. Reiden spat a tooth onto the floor in a spray of blood.

'Yes they do.'

'Then they shall be taught a lesson in due course. Right now, it's time for yours. Comments such as these, harmless though they seem, are in fact the foundations upon which dissent and rebellion are built. Words cannot be unsaid, Reiden. You can't deny that you really did imagine yourself as king. You can't deny that you really do doubt Commander Ostion. And if enough people start to doubt him, one of them will take it upon themselves to replace him or usurp him, and then starts a bloody, pointless rebellion all because *you* implied he was losing his touch. These harmless speculations and general observations of yours are just what's needed to start a rebellion. And that is as good as treason.'

'Treason? I never meant anything harmful.'

'Whether you did or didn't is irrelevant. All I know is that those words have been said and people are starting to believe them, even if they don't know it yet; the subconscious is a funny thing, Reiden. Unpredictable. It stores information and conceives concepts you never even thought it knew about. Your comments have undoubtedly sparked dissent in people's subconscious. But if you turn up the next day having been subject to the Segrata, that little spark of dissent in the subconscious suddenly goes out and everything is back to normal. Everybody will see what happened to you, and they will be scared, and the kingdom will be safe again.'

'No kingdom can be safe with terrorists like you around.'

'Terrorists?' Keph lowered his voice. 'You have guts, Reiden. Shall I spill them? Eh? Shall I spill those guts of yours?'

'At least it would leave a mess for you to clean up.'

'I'm not the one who has to clean up,' Keph said, drawing the sword and placing the tip against Reiden's chest, directly over his heart. He applied the pressure with practised gentleness, piercing the skin a millimetre at a time. A solitary tear of blood dribbled down Reiden's chest, followed a moment later by another as Keph pushed the blade fractionally deeper, and then a steady stream when Keph removed the sword entirely.

'Is that it?' Reiden said defiantly. 'Is that the extent of the Segrata's cruelty?'

'Not by a long shot,' Keph answered, moving the sword tip to the soft muscle at the front of Reiden's shoulder and making a sharp incision. He drove the point inwards with more force than before, twisting it savagely and drawing a pained gasp from his victim.

He drew it out swiftly.

'There's more to come yet,' he said.

'What if I say I don't want anymore?' Reiden demanded. 'What if I suddenly give up and give in to your terms?'

'Whether you've given in yet is irrelevant. I will finish this when I think you have taken enough. You need to be in such a state that people will see how dangerous . . . and how potentially fatal . . . it can be to cross the Segrata. You will be that message, Reiden. You will be the message from us to the people that the Segrata are not to be defied or denied, and that message must be convincing.'

He backhanded Reiden's nose with the sword hilt, before immediately swinging it back across again. Each of the cracks ricocheted off the walls, and a steady stream of blood began to pour from the remains of his nose.

'You're heartless vermin, all of you!' Reiden spat. Keph slammed his fist across his jaw again, but Reiden continued amid Keph's constant retaliations. 'You're all cowards, hiding . . . hiding your faces . . . And you're all no better than the king –' He spat out a second tooth as Keph's onslaught carried on unabated. 'The king is a monster . . . and a murderer . . . and a damn coward! He's only . . . he's only satisfied when he knows everyone who hates him is dead or driven insane by constant torture.'

Keph's boot crunched into his kneecap, breaking it with a sickening snap. Reiden roared in pain, but resumed his rant through gritted, bloody teeth.

'You're no better than criminals! You . . . you take people off the streets and break them . . . break them . . . until they're nothing but . . . but an empty shell. Nothing . . . nothing left except pain and . . . and misery and . . . we all hate you! We hate you! You . . . you barbarians took . . . you took my sons from me! You took them, and they came back two days later, and there was nothing left of them! I looked into their eyes and I saw nothing! Nothing! They were boys, damn it! Boys! Not yet eighteen, and you broke them! Those are wounds that will never heal. Never. You have scarred those boys – my boys –for life, and for what? Tell me that. Tell me that!'

His words were left ringing in the silence as Keph stood quietly, sword lowered. His grip on it faltered, and it nearly dropped from his hand, but he reasserted control over his body and gripped the hilt firmly.

Reiden smiled grimly.

'Heh. Struck a nerve, eh? Has old Vict Reiden rattled the Segrata?'

Keph made a decision quickly, knowing both that he could not turn back once he had made it, and that it was wrong – morally wrong – and yet necessity told him it was right and justified.

'Wounds that will never heal, you say?' he said slowly. 'Aye, that's us. That's what we do to people who defy us, who mock us, who defy the king. You're no exception. Now, I'm no surgeon. I'm no doctor, no physician. But I do know the importance of an eye. Important things, eyes. Vulnerable too. Right in the front of your head . . . where everyone can see them, unless of course your own have already been put out.' He paused, idly tracing a circle on the stone floor with the sword tip. 'What? Nothing to say now? No fiery defiance? Has the Segrata rattled old Vict Reiden?'

'What are you going to do to me?'

His voice had changed. There was nothing left in it anymore. It was broken, cracked, and tired. But Keph had started down this path now. He would not . . . could not . . . stop until it was over. To do that would be to prove the Segrata's weakness, and therefore the king's weakness. If there was one thing Keph had resolved never to do, it was to betray the king.

'What am I going to do? I'll tell you what I'm going to do.' He raised Reiden's chin with the tip of his sword so that from underneath the hood he was eye to eye with his prisoner. Not that Reiden knew they were eye to eye. 'I'm going to make sure that when you return to work in the kitchens tomorrow morning, everyone there will know that you have been in our company. They will see these bruises on your chest –'

He thumped his fist into Reiden's ribcage. Something snapped, and Reiden screamed.

'– and on your stomach –'

Reiden screamed again.

'– and they will see your blooded, broken nose and your snapped and shattered teeth –'

He slammed the sword hilt into Reiden's face. Something cracked, and more blood spattered onto the floor.

'– and they will see the scars on your shoulders –'

He drove his sword into one shoulder, then the other, the keen blade sliding between sinew and bone with cruel ease, then sliced neatly into Reiden's upper arm, drawing yet another stream of blood.

'– and they will see the remains of your eye –'

He filtered out the agonised screaming and the bloody mess that followed.

'– and they will know fear.'

Chapter 5.

Baron Gadric and his retinue were due to arrive that evening, and the king ordered that the kitchens provide the very best for the baron. He even went so far as to tell the cooks to use the boar that he himself had shot two days before. Cassien was taking no chances with Gadric.

Fear was taking control.

It was taking control so much that Cassien supervised the preparations personally, from the bedrooms in the south wing to the food in the kitchens. He walked round and tasted every dish until he was satisfied, and then made sure it was properly stored so that it could be served the moment the baron arrived. The presence of the king made everything seem that little bit more important; not so much that the servants were flustered, but just enough that they kept working until everything was perfect.

As the day progressed, and the preparations continued, the air got warmer, until by early afternoon the sun was bright and the clouds were starting to pass overhead. The approach to the city was watched constantly, waiting for the arrival of Gadric and his retinue. More than once the king made his way to the main gate to watch for himself, but his agitation prevented him from staying in one place too long. He came and went from the guest quarters and the kitchens and the city gates so frequently it seemed as though he was always there, and yet always gone at the same time.

And in amongst everything, Deel stood in the middle of the palace courtyard with a quill, a bottle of ink, and scores of sheets of paper. He had found a balcony on the east wing and was writing his aptly named *Balcony Scene* with furious abandon, continually shouting phrases of love and adoration up to the balcony itself.

The passing soldiers decided he had finally gone insane.

He became even more animated when he looked up to find that the balcony belonged to the Lady Jessa. Between them they wrote, read, rewrote and reread the lines, him never leaving the courtyard and her never leaving the balcony. The poet scribbled and muttered, scratching his head every other word and looking about him constantly, whilst on the balcony Jessa leant down with her dark hair blowing in the breeze and an amused smile playing on her lips. The whole ridiculousness of it made even Cassien smile among his fears and worries.

'Don't overdo yourself, Deel,' he warned. 'My ward can be a bit feisty sometimes.'

'My liege, I would never . . . I was . . . a play, my liege. My next great work! A romance, my liege, a romance! So beautiful and so tragic! Star-crossed lovers from rival families – '

'And a sleeping draught too, no doubt,' Cassien chuckled. 'A dirty trick with a sleeping draught. If you can include that into a pathetic romance I'll put fifty crowns towards its production. That will be fifty crowns from my own pocket, mark you.'

'My liege? Are you serious? I mean – '

'I am. And if you can include a spontaneous friar as well, I'll give you a hundred crowns.'

He walked on briskly, muttering to himself.

'Lovers from rival families. What will the man think of next? He's ridiculous and yet brilliant at the same time. How does he do it?'

He left a stunned Deel in his wake. It was only by Jessa's urging that he was able to continue with his *Balcony Scene* and not get caught up in Cassien's challenge for the rest of the play.

As the day drew to a close, and evening grew closer, the men of Bronze Keep were spotted riding towards the city. The gates were opened and the road to the palace emptied of citizens. A small delegation of palace guard escorted the baron and his men through the city to the palace, where Cassien awaited with Alsarra, Jessa, Commander Ostion, Fadrinar, and the rest of his ministers.

It was a warm reception from the king, but on Gadric's side the response was cold and terse.

'Welcome to Sorl, baron,' said Cassien. 'I appreciate your coming. It is too long since we met as friends.'

'I assure you, sire, that is through no fault of mine,' Gadric replied coldly. He was older than Keph had expected, but still lean and strong enough to sit at ease in the saddle. It was hard to guess his exact age, but it was clear enough in his retinue who his sons were, and who his grandson was. The two sons looked in their mid-forties, one big and broad and the other somewhat stouter. The grandson was tall and rangy, with a weathered face and young features. At a guess, Keph would have said he was no more than twenty.

The rest of the retinue was similarly unresponsive. They sat tall and still in their saddles, donned in full armour and wearing a sword, knife and shield each.

The gardener from the Segrata appeared at Keph's shoulder and whispered, 'It certainly looks like they've come to fight.'

Keph noticed that Fadrinar and Commander Ostion were eyeing the soldiers with similar looks of distrust on their faces. Cassien, if he thought the same thing, was masterful enough to keep it hidden behind his big brown beard.

'I never said it was your fault,' he returned. 'It is merely the circumstances that have not been favourable towards us.'

'Quite,' Gadric said. Then, 'I believe you have met my sons before.'

'Yes, I remember,' said Cassien. 'Princes Borden and Locan, if I remember.' He looked at each as he said their names. Prince Borden, the stouter and elder of the two, responded with a courteous bow from horseback, but Locan, the larger one, dipped his chin stiffly. 'But I do not believe I have met your grandson,' Cassien continued.

'No, you have not. My liege, may I present Prince Talan, son of Prince Borden.'

The rangy prince walked his horse forward and performed a similar bow to his father's. It was not all for Cassien though; his body bowed to Cassien, but his eyes were fixed on Jessa, who seemed similarly intent on fixing her eyes on him. Keph looked briefly to Fadrinar, and saw that the commissar too had noticed this and was stroking his chin with his thumb.

'It's an honour, my liege,' said Talan. For such a young man his voice was deep and mellow.

'Likewise,' said Cassien. 'May I present my niece and ward, Lady Jessa.'

Jessa, with her eyes still fixed firmly on Prince Talan, curtsied quickly and smiled.

'I heard your brother was a good man, sire,' Gadric said. 'I was sorry to hear of his death.'

'It can happen to the best of us,' Cassien replied. 'Though in some ways I am thankful; I have been left with perhaps the most desirable young lady in the kingdom to give away as I please.'

Both Jessa and Talan looked sharply at Cassien, but he seemed not to notice.

'Baron,' said Queen Alsarra. 'You must be tired. The south wing has been prepared for you. You will find a warm meal and warm beds waiting for you. Commander Ostion, please escort our guests to their quarters.'

'Would you care to join me for a little breakfast tomorrow morning?' Cassien added as Ostion led most of the retinue towards the southern wing of the palace. 'Perhaps a bit of shooting just beyond the city gates.'

The force and directness of his words made it clear that it would be unwise of Gadric to refuse his offer. After all, how could one refuse a king his sport?

'I am afraid I'm not much one for sport, sire,' Gadric said deftly. 'Although Borden, despite his bulk, is an avid rider and has a keen eye with a crossbow. Perhaps he would like to join you.'

'I would consider it my privilege,' Borden said.

'Wonderful,' said Cassien. Shall we say half past seven? We can spend a few hours riding and shooting and be back for lunch and diplomatic discussion at one.'

'I would be delighted, sire,' Borden said, smiling disarmingly.

The guests were led to their rooms, and the servants from the south wing waited on them. Keph returned to work cooking for the king and his family in the north wing. Once again, he was approached by Deel after the final course and told about how the play was progressing.

'A veritable tragedy!' the poet kept saying. 'It will have them weeping by the end, mark my words. Weeping! It may even get a tear from the king, though I doubt he'll show it. And Lady Jessa has been most helpful. The scene on the balcony is complete, as are the majority of the early scenes. The later ones are coming along nicely too. Now all I need are some actors to do the deed and play the parts. I would go for the cast of my previous one, but they've gone touring the countryside. I could wait, but they won't be back for another year. Marvellous stuff, marvellous!' he cried, juggling a trio of spoons as he spoke. 'Such revolutionary work, such grand ideas and innovative, daring staging. Mark my words, Keph, mark my words: the next few days will see the start of a new era!'

Chapter 6.

Keph made his way to the kitchens early the next morning to prepare a few small snacks for Cassien and Prince Borden to take on their hunting trip, as was his duty when the king was due to be away from the city for any length of time. Quite why the king was risking leaving the city while Gadric and two thousand soldiers were housed in his palace was beyond Keph. But he was sure there was a reason; if there wasn't, why was Cassien doing it?

He was not the only person in the kitchens, however. Vict Reiden was there too, a pair of wooden crutches propped next to him, eating what seemed to be an early breakfast. The day was new, the light was different, and he didn't look as bad as he had done during Keph's interrogation. But then, there had been a lot of blood and bone to take into consideration, not to mention the eye itself. There was a patch covering the socket now, thankfully.

'Morning, Vict.'

'Morning, Keph. You're down early.'

'So are you.'

'Couldn't sleep. Damn body aches all over.'

'What happened to you yesterday? We struggled to cope without you, what with all the preparations for the baron's arrival.'

'Yesterday? Segrata picked me up yesterday morning. Didn't let me go till sundown.'

'Segrata? They took you of all people?'

'Aye, they took me. Took me for the things I said a couple of days ago, about Ostion and the king. Thought it was rebellious. Put my eye out, among other things.'

'Good Gods!' said Keph, feigning horror. 'They don't give up. You yesterday, they took Pelk on Monday. You know Alster, the carpenter? Practically broke him last week.'

'They're brutal,' said Reiden, nodding.

Brutal, yes, Keph thought to himself. *But also necessary. I had hoped that you would understand that now.*

'Yes, they are brutal,' he said aloud. 'But why did they do so much to you just for implying things?'

'Seem to think everyone's got it in the back of their minds now that rebelling might be a good idea. All because of me wondering things. I wouldn't rebel, not in a thousand years. Don't know how to. Have to wait for someone else to start and then just tag along. But I don't know a thing about ruling, about making laws and things like that. I'd never rebel, and yet they still do this to me.'

'Perhaps they thought that if enough people see you like this they might fall back in line again.'

'They why not hang me from a gibbet and cut my heart out and put it on a damn flagpole and march through the city waving it? No, it's more fun for them to torment me like this. Like I said, they're brutal. And cowards.'

'Cowards?' *We're anything but cowards; we're the only ones willing to take on this gritty job.*

'Aye, cowards, the lot of them. All dark rooms and cloaks and hoods that hide their faces. Don't even know who it was that did this to me. If I did I'd – '

'Kill them? Take revenge? Even I wouldn't kill a Segrata member; too many consequences. Nasty consequences. More nasty than losing an eye, I'd wager.'

'Not a fighter at heart are you, Keph? Always knew you lacked courage. Say . . . you're not Segrata are you?'

Reiden leaned forwards, peering into Keph's face the same way he had peered under Keph's hood the day before.

'Me? You've seen the way I cut a piece of beef. Can you imagine me trying to take someone's eye out all by myself? Besides, how can you call me a coward when I'm one of the few people in this kitchen willing to face the king on a daily basis?'

Reiden was silent for a moment, then grunted somewhat grudgingly.

'Point taken.'

'Will you be alright?' Keph asked. 'The eye and all that?'

'Well, I'm not dead. At least they didn't do that to me. Lost a few teeth though, not to mention the eye, broken knee and broken nose. They ought to be fine soon. I'll struggle through, even if it is on crutches. They may have broken me, but I ain't beat yet.'

'That's good to hear,' Keph said truthfully. *At least I wasn't as cruel as some others would have been.* 'You could be a lot worse off.' *You should count yourself lucky it was me and not another agent. Another would have made sure you were worse off.*

'You're not the first to tell me that. And you won't be the last either.' Reiden scooped the last crumbs off his plate. 'So why are you down so early?'

'The king and Prince Borden are going hunting this morning. I'm preparing a few things for them.'

'Just in case they don't bag anything, eh?'

'Something like that.'

'Need a hand?'

'Don't trouble yourself. I can manage.'

'I was hoping you'd say that.'

Keph began to prepare the food and store it in a couple of small wicker baskets. Reiden spoke again after a brief silence.

'Baron brought a lot of soldiers with him. Almost like he wants to intimidate the king.'

'The king is not a man who is easily intimidated,' Keph replied.

'No, but nor is the baron from what I hear. Going to be like two bulls locking horns and messing up everything underneath them. I may not be into my old age yet, Keph, but let me tell you I got that feeling in my bones all the old men talk about. Just before the storm. We got one on the way, take my word. This won't end without someone getting killed.'

'You seem very sure.'

'You never got a bad feeling before?'

Yes. About a month after I joined the Segrata.

'No.'

'Well in that case, take my word. Once this storm breaks there's going to be violence. And it won't just be the ones at the top who start getting killed.'

'The eye of the storm is often the safest place, Vict,' said Keph. 'So once everything gets going, stay close to the king. The safest place to be will be by his side.'

'And that's where you'll be, I take it?'

'Absolutely.'

'Faithful little rat aren't you?'

Keph smiled.

'Something like that.'

The kitchen door opened, and the king's Hunt Master limped in, a loaded crossbow slung on his back. He ignored Reiden and spoke only to Keph.

'The king wants you to join him in the hunting party, but I'll be damned if I know why. There's a horse saddled and waiting for you, if you know how to ride. If not, you'll learn. Quickly. The nobles are assembled in the courtyard; don't keep them waiting.'

He departed as briskly as he had come.

'Well,' Reiden mocked. 'Someone's moving in high circles, aren't they? Going hunting with the king. So when's he making you a duke, eh?'

'I don't know any more than you do, Vict.'

'And that's very comforting. Put in a good word for me, will you? Maybe I'll be a count by the end of the year. Heh. Who am I kidding? Well, run along, Keph. Don't keep the nobs waiting.'

Chapter 7.

When Keph arrived at the courtyard with a pair of wicker baskets of food, the hunting party was indeed ready and waiting for him. Though it appeared the dogs and the beaters has already been dispatched, half a dozen of the king's ministers remained, clad in rustic greens and browns. Prince Borden sat among them, talking amiably, his horse always moving, always restless. The king's valet was in close attendance to Cassien, who himself was in deep conversation with the young, lean Hunt Master, but sat suddenly upright upon Keph's arrival.

'Ah!' he said brightly. 'If it isn't the best cook in my kingdom. Come and ride with us. I wouldn't have anyone else look after my food for me. This young man here is the very essence of cookery, Borden. Did you have the boar last night? Cooked to perfection by Keph here. I don't know all my servants by name, but Keph deserves special attention because of his special skills. I would have him promoted to head chef, but he doesn't have the sort of voice to keep everyone on task. Much too demure, aren't you, boy? Anyway, let's go. Things to shoot, talks to have.'

The king set a rapid pace, out of the palace and through the city to the main gate. Once outside the city, they turned south towards a small woodland. Keph had never properly learned to ride, but he had found that on the few horse journeys he had made, he was not such a bad rider. There were, however, problems he still encountered. To take his mind off them he turned his brain to working out what Cassien was playing at, accepting a dissident noble and accompanying army into his palace and then leaving with said noble's eldest son.

And his manner was odd too. Keph would readily admit he did not know the king nearly as well as some others did, but it was rare indeed for him to be lively and friendly, especially to the extent that caused him and his rival's heir to go hunting together.

They dismounted at the wood's edge and the Hunt Master led the nobles further in, the beaters and dogs ahead of him. Keph and the king's valet were left with the food and the horses.

'I know we've both been with the Segrata a while,' the valet said once the nobles were out of sight, 'and I know your name is Keph, but I don't know if you know mine. I would say it was unfair if that were the case. I'm Nard.' He held out his hand.

'Good to meet you properly,' said Keph, taking it firmly. 'Do you have any idea what the king's doing, coming all the way out here with the prince?'

'None at all,' replied Nard. 'But he doesn't normally take cooks with him on these rare hunting trips. I think you're here because you're Segrata.'

'But you're Segrata too. Why bring me as well?'

'Two pairs of eyes, two pairs of ears, two more sword arms if it should ever come to that. Two Segrata agents are better than one, especially in times like these.'

'Is the king scared?'

'I can't be sure. I've been his servant since he turned eighteen, and while I have known him to act strangely, he has always had a valid reason. For this behaviour, however, I can find no explanation. I wish sometimes that he would tell me more than he does, but he is becoming secretive nowadays. I have known him to be many things, Keph, but scared is not one of them. Besides, what can Prince Borden do out here? He's surrounded by the king and his ministers.'

'I'm more worried about back in the city,' Keph said. 'With the king out of the way, Gadric can do whatever he likes.'

'The baron will not act hastily. He is a shrewd, calculating man. I do not think he comes here to settle his differences with the king. I think he is here to take over by force – an armed rebellion in the palace itself – and he wants to do it as soon as possible. He also knows the king fairly well though, and it is well known that the king is not much of a sportsman. I believe the baron was expecting to be able to start his takeover first thing this morning, before he had to endure the talks over lunch. In fact, that might be the reason the king is doing this: he has done something Gadric did not expect, and removed one of his key pieces – Prince Borden – in one movement.'

'Gadric will not only want the city,' Keph said slowly, starting to catch on, 'but the king too. If he takes the city but the king is out here, we can escape somewhere else and bring back an army. Gadric can't make his move with the king outside the city.'

'My thoughts exactly.' Nard glanced over his shoulder into the trees. 'I know the king has very little political savvy, but I think he is more cunning than we give him credit for. He may not know how to keep people happy, but he knows how to deal with those who aren't.'

'He plays a dangerous game to do it though,' Keph said.

'He does,' agreed Nard. 'But that's why we are here.'

'Surely if the dissidents were going to try something like this it would make more sense for someone like Cardil to do it, being much more of a soldier than Gadric,' Keph remarked.

'Cardil may be more suited to the action,' said Nard, 'but Gadric is more patient, and more able to turn things to his advantage before making a move. He would also see it as his duty to do it; after all, he and the king have . . . history between them.'

'History? What do you mean?'

'You don't know?' Nard seemed surprised. 'I don't feel it's my place to tell you, Segrata or no. It is not something the king speaks of often. It is perhaps the most controversial decision he has ever made, and he has bidden me not to speak of it. I will not betray his trust in me.'

'I would never ask you to,' said Keph. Nevertheless, his curiosity was aroused.

Their conversation drifted into silence, and soon they heard the nobles coming back through the wood. The rustle of the first autumn leaves was clear and crisp in the silence. When he appeared, Cassien seemed quite pleased, and Borden, it appeared, was content.

'You have a keen eye, sire,' Borden said to Cassien. 'I wonder that you do not sport more often than you do.'

'When I know that my kingdom is safe,' Cassien replied, looking directly at Borden, 'perhaps then I will be able to take up more sport. Until that time, I believe I shall have to be content with what I can get. Besides, you have a much keener eye than I do. What was it? Eighty paces you shot that thing from? In a dense woodland too. Remarkable.'

'Thank you, sire, but I think the largest kill of the day belongs to you. That boar was larger than any near Bronze Keep.'

'We breed them well around here.'

'Do you indeed? I should like to learn how.'

'Perhaps when we have a little more time,' Cassien said evasively. 'If you wish to learn something from the best, why don't you remain here and let Keph show you how to prepare a beast like this? He is truly a master of his art.'

Borden was silent. He looked over to Keph, clearly calculating something.

'Very well,' he said. 'Why not?'

'Excellent,' smiled Cassien. 'Let's go for another circuit, see if we can find the injured one.'

The party left their catches with the horses, and disappeared into the wood again, leaving Keph and Nard with Borden. It was Borden who spoke first.

'Does the king mean what he says about you and your art?'

'He means well,' replied Keph, 'but I am afraid I'm not as good as he gives me credit for. I'm a cook in the kitchens. There's not much to it. Not as much as with sword fighting or hunting or being a noble.'

'The king seems to value a simple cook very highly,' Borden remarked. His tone may have been casual, but it was clearly laced with suspicion.

'The simple cooks are often the most reliable,' Keph said. 'As is the way with most servants, I find. Take Nard,' he said, indicating the valet. 'He does his job with efficiency and never does anything above what he should.'

'Fair enough,' said Borden. 'So, how would you prepare a boar then? Let me learn from the supposed master.'

It was a slower process than usual, and unexpectedly so; Keph was not expecting the number of questions that Borden asked him, both about the boar, about the king, about the city, and about himself. Nard spoke where he could to alleviate the pressure on Keph, but it was clear Borden was more interested in getting Keph to talk than allowing Nard to.

'And what about Lady Jessa?' asked Borden. 'What is she like?'

'Many of the men in the court get more than they bargain for when trying to win her.' Keph adjusted the knife in his hand and moved on to the next piece of boar. 'She likes her independence, and is determined to marry who she wants, when she wants. I do not like to speak ill of my superiors, but there is no doubt about her lack of respect for the king's authority. She is the best of all the ladies in Sorl, or so the rumours go, but she has a number of drawbacks that make her slightly less desirable on closer acquaintance.'

'Indeed? She dislikes the king so much?'

The direction of his question was clear: he wanted to know if he could get Lady Jessa on his side.

'I would not say that she dislikes the king,' replied Keph. 'But I think she resents her position. If not for her father's death she would be in the family estate in the Grey Hills, free to do as she pleased most of the time. But being the king's ward and niece has resulted in her being practically confined to the palace. Her rebellious streak has resulted in her quarters being moved away from the north wing. She is now situated in the east.'

'Interesting,' said Borden. 'I knew a young lady once, who lived in her father's estate so far out she never met anyone to marry, solely because nobody travelled that way.'

'Out of interest, sir,' said Keph, eager both to try to change the subject and to find out about the *history* Nard had mentioned, 'what is the reason for your father's disagreement with the king?'

'It's an old feud, going back a couple of decades. To be honest, I'm surprised you don't know the particulars; it seems more people know nowadays than should know.'

'News tends not to filter down to the kitchens,' Keph replied.

'That does surprise me,' said Borden. 'In Bronze Keep, the servants seem to know things before we do. But perhaps our servants are kept on a slightly longer leash than you are. Regarding the king and my father, it is a rather delicate matter.'

'I can do delicate,' said Keph. 'Besides, I'm not really in a position to affect it, am I?'

'No, I suppose not. I will keep it brief though; I doubt the king would like it if he were to come back to find me talking to you about him and my father. But I'm a fair man. You deserve to know what everyone else seems to know.'

The prince took a glance over his shoulder into the wood, then turned back to Keph and Nard.

'Twenty years ago, Sorl was at war with Andaria. The king used my father to win the war, but it was a deceptive and cruel ploy. I won't go into details, but from the deployment of the Andarian army it was clear that we could not afford to leave our camp exposed. Andarian cavalry are faster than one would expect, and more ruthless than our own. Being not so far out of Sorl, the king was willing to risk leaving the camp exposed so that more troops could be diverted to attack the Andarian army itself. My father and I, and a number of other generals, warned him that exposing the camp would mean the loss of the army's food, water, shelter, and support.

'Eventually, we succeeded in persuading him not to expose the camp. Or so we thought. From the hill on the far side of our army, I saw the king give the order for the troops defending the camp to join the battle line. The moment he did so, the Andarian cavalry was attacking around the flank. They torched the camp and hit the rear of the army. The king was clearly expecting it, and turned a couple of companies to face the cavalry, utterly destroying them.

'Ultimately, we won. We broke the back of the Andarian army and forced a surrender and a peace treaty, but the army then had to travel home with no food, water or shelter. Almost a third of the men died on the way home, even with rationing what we had managed to salvage. It was a victory, but it cost more lives than it should have. The king was brutal, ruthless. He allowed his army's support to be destroyed and the countless people maintaining it killed. He won the battle, and the war, but the way in which he did it lost him the support of my father and half a dozen other noble families. It hurt my father in particular, because it was his men that the king ordered away from the camp.'

'It seems like such a small thing to disagree over,' Nard remarked. 'The battle was won, I was there. It was decisive.'

'It was decisive,' agreed Borden. 'But the way the king won the battle was immoral. He did not have to sacrifice those people, but he did. He sacrificed defenceless people and the whole support train for his army so that his victory could be huge and decisive. He could easily have won without letting those people die, but he didn't. It was this that lost him our support; it was his willingness to throw away countless lives for his own ease and glory. A king who acts like that does not deserve his title.'

'Then why has your father decided to come and talk about it after so long?' asked Keph. 'Why is he going to talk about it instead of raising an army of his own and dethroning the king?'

'Is this rebellious talk I hear?' said a loud voice behind them. 'Will I have to set my Segrata on you, Keph?'

'No, sire,' Keph replied, turning and bowing to Cassien.

'Glad to hear it. May I have a word with you?' Cassien said, though it was a request that could hardly be refused.

Keph approached the king, who took him silently towards the edge of the wood.

'Congratulations, Keph,' the king said. 'I knew there was a good reason for bringing you along. Borden has just admitted that Gadric wants me removed, and it was through your questioning that he admitted it. I doubt the baron brought two thousand men because he expected it to be peaceful. No, Gadric is going to start a rebellion not out in the villages with his dissident friends, but inside my own palace. It's genius. But he has not taken you and the rest of the Segrata into account. I am going to give you to Borden as a gift; you and he seem to get on well enough, and I want a reliable man inside the baron's inner circle.'

'What for, sire?'

'You are going to gather every scrap of information you can about Gadric's rebellion. We may have less men than he does, and his men are trained and hardened soldiers. But we do have the Segrata on our side. I believe we can defeat Gadric, but we must be on our guard. I want you inside, so that you can do what you do best, whatever that may be.'

'Very well, sire. I will do what I can.'

'I know you will. That will not happen quite yet though. I expect Gadric to keep to the agreements of a talk this lunchtime; I won't leave him any choice. You will be serving the food, as usual. After that, you will report to Borden's service. I shall inform Commissar Fadrinar and the baron of the development.'

Chapter 8.

As predicted, Baron Gadric kept his word and attended the lunch served by Cassien's 'best servants'. It seemed that the king was trying to maintain the illusion that he was ignorant of Gadric's intentions, and he did it extremely well: there was everything that would be expected of a large meal and diplomatic discussion between noble families.

The food was cooked to perfection, the best wine was chosen to fill the glasses, and even the seating was perfect. Cassien at one end, with Alsarra down the other. Down the table to Cassien's right sat Jessa, Gadric and Talan, and down to his left were Borden, Locan and Commander Ostion. The commander was present at Cassien's wish to fill up the numbers. He was clearly out of place, which was undoubtedly why he was seated so far from the king.

Even Deel had been persuaded to emerge from his mountains of scrapped and redrafted papers, discarded quills and scenes of romance and drama to provide light relief from behind the right hand side of Cassien's chair. He made witty remarks on the conversation, and recited a few lines of verse when necessary.

As for Keph, he was stood at the side of the large room, always watching for an empty glass or plate, as well as for anything suspicious. Guards were stationed around the room. Some were Commander Ostion's men, and some were Gadric's men. Among Ostion's men, Jerl was the most senior. It was from next to his brother that Keph decided he would watch and wait.

'What do you think?' Jerl said.

'I think it's all too elaborate,' replied Keph. 'Why is he spending so much time and effort on this lunch when he could have had the discussion this morning? I don't quite understand.'

A chorus of laughs from the table drew his attention, and he looked over to see Deel capering around, seemingly imitating a bird of some kind.

'It beats me why the baron is going along with it,' added Jerl. 'But then, this is politics. I never understood it.'

'Me neither,' said Keph. 'But I get the feeling we'll both be learning very quickly.'

'Really, Deel!' Cassien laughed. 'You do surprise me sometimes!'

'Always glad to be of service, my liege.'

'How is your play progressing, Deel?' asked Jessa.

'Ah, yes.' Cassien's interruption was so forceful it took even Deel by surprise. 'How is the great work? Have you taken on my challenge?'

'I have, my liege,' Deel answered quickly. 'I believe I have done it. I will finish it this afternoon and then give it to your eminence to read this evening, if you so desire.'

'I do, most certainly. I shall even have my purse with me.'

'Do you take much of an interest in theatre, sire?' asked Borden.

'Not as much as my wife. She adores it, don't you, Alsarra?'

'Definitely,' the queen replied. 'I find sometimes that helping my husband rule a kingdom is tiresome work. I can think of no man better than our Deel to reduce life's hardships by so much that they almost disappear.'

'Until the next morning, of course,' Deel added. 'When it all comes flooding back.'

'I try not to think about that,' Alsarra said. 'You do have a most remarkable talent though.'

'I beg you do not judge me so, my queen . . . till you my greatest yet romance have seen.'

Among the subsequent applause, the poet smiled, took a bow, and spread his arms, indicating it was somebody else's turn to carry the conversation. Surprisingly, Prince Locan had not been listening to the talk about theatre, but was in deep conversation with Commander Ostion. The old commander appeared slightly reserved in his comments. Keph noticed Locan's almost empty wine glass and made his way over to refill it and stack some empty dishes nearby.

'I tend to find a longer blade more practical,' Locan was saying. 'I find I can get more swing behind it.'

'You have little finesse, it seems, when it comes to anything,' Ostion observed. 'You tell me about your dislike for politics, and yet even with a sword you are very blunt. If I didn't know better, I would have said that the king himself had taught you how to rule.'

Locan seized on this statement.

'You dislike the king?'

'I never said that,' Ostion replied. 'I was merely stating how similar you both are. The king too is a direct and forthright man. He gets what he wants.'

'I see,' Locan said slowly. 'How do you train your men? Do you have them drill, or are you a theorist soldier?'

'I show them what works and doesn't work, and why. But I will readily admit my men are not as well trained or disciplined as yours. After all, yours are part of a standing army. Mine are merely guardsmen. They don't have the same discipline as yours.'

'I'm sure you're being too modest, commander.'

Despite this comment, Locan seemed satisfied with the result of his conversation. It turned from the soldiers to past battles. There was one battle that the two of them had clearly both been present at, but which they never mentioned.

On his way back to the door to the kitchens, Keph caught a glimpse of Prince Talan, who was leaning back contentedly in his chair, his large hands behind his head, looking up the table towards Jessa. Once or twice her gaze flickered to him, but nothing more.

After leaving the empty dishes in the kitchens, Keph returned to stand with Jerl and watch the subsequent proceedings.

'Now then, baron,' Cassien said briskly. 'I think we ought to finally get down to business. You have made an impressive display with all your soldiers and your cold manners, but I will not be intimidated. We both know that you hate me, and we both know why. I know nothing can ever go back to the way it was before our disagreement, but I want to settle things once and for all. The relations between our families have been strained to say the least, and I believe that both of us would benefit from a restoration of civility between us.'

'If you have something to say,' Gadric said, 'then damn well say it. I didn't come here to exchange pleasantries and fancy words. Now what is it you're trying to say?'

'I propose a union between our two families. A marriage. Lady Jessa and Prince Talan.'

Both Jessa and Talan looked stunned, though Keph was sure he was not the only one to notice a certain lack of protest from them.

'I have no heir,' Cassien continued. 'And both Alsarra and I think it's too late to produce one now. As my only living relative, Jessa will inherit Sorl. When that happens, she will need a good, strong husband to be her king. I can think of nothing better than to mend the rift between our families by giving your grandson the inheritance a man of his calibre deserves.'

Keph could see the beginnings of a smirk behind Cassien's heavy beard. Once again, the king had outplayed Gadric. Surely the baron wanted to take over not for personal reasons, but to secure what *he believed* was a better future for the generations yet to come. The throne would eventually have worked its way through Borden, and then on to Talan. If Talan married Jessa, he would get the throne substantially quicker than if he had to wait for two generations to pass him by.

Gadric was clearly stumped, as were his sons. None of them had expected Cassien to propose giving Jessa to Talan. The prince himself had clearly hoped for a proposal of this nature, but the surprise on his face made it clear he had never actually expected it to happen.

Keph could see Deel's mind working on a way to break the silence with something amusing, but even Deel's quick wit could not provide him with anything suitable enough.

'My kingdom means a lot to me,' said Cassien. 'It always has. I have always wanted what is best for it, and what is best for my niece. She has never truly been satisfied with her place in the world, but when she succeeds me I hope she will understand why I have done what I have. I cannot think of a man I would rather see succeed me as king than your grandson, baron.'

That too was the genius of the king's proposal: by marrying off Jessa to Talan, the throne would completely bypass Gadric and Borden. The king knew it would be hard to completely crush Gadric's rebellion by force, so he was trying to defuse it somehow, catch Gadric of his guard with something.

'You hardly know my grandson,' the baron said slowly. 'How do you know he is the one you want to succeed you?'

'Because he is descended from one of the best nobles I have ever met.'

'And that's the killer,' Jerl muttered. 'It's masterful work, Keph. He's got him now.'

Keph didn't reply. He was too busy studying the people at the table.

'Prince Talan appears at first to be a gentleman,' Locan said. 'But he is rash and impetuous. I doubt he would make for a great king. Not until he has been taught properly.'

'My niece can be a wonderful teacher,' said Cassien smoothly. 'She will make him a proper gentleman in no time.'

'I notice the two young people whom this concerns have not yet spoken,' Gadric said. He turned his gaze to Talan. 'Perhaps it is worth hearing what they have to say?'

'I don't really know what I can say,' said Talan. 'It would be rude to refuse immediately, and yet presumptuous to immediately accept. I don't think this is something that can be decided here and now.'

Which is exactly why the king has said it here and now, Keph said to himself. *If you can't make a decision until later, it postpones any other plans you have even further. The problem comes if Gadric decides to be bull headed enough to carry on with his plans without considering this other option.*

'When I marry,' Jessa said, looking straight down the table at Talan, 'I want it to be because I love him, and he loves me. I cannot accept my uncle's proposition until I have proof of the prince's feelings one way or another.'

'It could take time for those feelings to develop, my dear,' Alsarra said. 'Your stubbornness could result in these negotiations taking too long. I doubt your uncle or the baron would look kindly on that.'

'On the contrary,' said Cassien. 'I want to be sure that everything is satisfactory for everyone. After all, that's why we're all here.'

'I agree that a marriage between my son and your niece would be advantageous,' said Borden, 'but I must agree with my brother: my son is rash and untested in the world. If any such union was to take place I would rather it occurred after he has a few more years of experience behind him.'

'I won't deny the immediate attractions of the prospect,' Talan said. 'And I would relish the opportunity to get to know the Lady Jessa better – her charms and her wit are more than desirable – but I cannot go against what my father has said.'

'If you are prepared to wait a few years,' said Jessa, 'then so am I. I won't exactly be going anywhere else.'

'A few years is too long!' Gadric snapped. 'I don't want this business to go on any longer than it has to. I'm not waiting a few years to see if my grandson is ready to marry yet, and I'm not having him giving in to his impulses and marrying your niece. The union is out of the question. You shall have to find another way to mend this rift, if that is what you really want us here for.'

'It's not about what I want you here for,' said Cassien. 'It's about what *you* are really here for.'

His cool, calculated gaze locked with Gadric's fiery glare. It was a full ten seconds before Gadric looked away.

'So,' he growled. 'What else do you have to offer me?'

'Various trade agreements, though I do not particularly want to place an economic value on our relationship. You, however, may be tempted to when you hear about my most recent trade partner.'

'How recent?'

'Within the last two weeks.'

'Who?'

'I have established a trade route – a safe trade route, mark you – with the Dashaar.'

Again, Keph caught a smirk behind Cassien's beard as Gadric's eyes widened.

'The Dashaar?' he said, clearly unconvinced. 'That's impossible. They haven't traded with the other kingdoms in decades.'

'I know,' Cassien grinned. 'That's why I have the signed agreement to show you.'

From inside his robes, the king produced a scroll. He opened it and began to read.

'By the command of King Bern of the Dashaar, the following trade agreements have been reached with King Cassien of Sorl: black powder for fifteen crowns per gram; iron mined from the Jade Peaks for ten shillings per gram (that's half the price Rhenar sell it for); and a full cohort of Dashaar Dragon Warriors for five hundred crowns. Signed by both King Bern and myself.'

He passed the document down to Gadric, who scanned it quickly, and then sat back and folded his arms.

'What can you offer me out of this?' he demanded.

'Half the iron, and two thirds of the black powder in exchange for twenty-five percent of the price I paid for it.'

'And what about the Dragon Warriors?'

'They stay with me, as my investment. If you, or indeed any of the other nobles, want their services, you will pay me eighty crowns. That will cover their maintenance and repairs, as well as giving me a profit. Eighty crowns for five hundred of the best fighters this side of the Jade Peaks is but a small inconvenience.'

Gadric chewed his lip thoughtfully.

'The amount we spend at the moment on iron from Rhenar is heavily taxing our treasury,' Borden said. 'If the king can get it at half the price, and if we can get it a quarter of that price – a full eighth of what we are currently paying – as well as a supply of black powder, our military capability would soon outstrip practically anyone else in the kingdom. It is a small expense, father, compared to what we are paying at the moment. Perhaps we really ought to consider it.'

'I agree that having the increase in military capability would be a big boost,' added Locan. 'The outlaws, when they band together, are crippling our soldiers as it stands right now, but more iron for vastly less money, as well as the ability to use more firearms, would give our citizens all the protection they need.'

'The princes make good points,' Jerl murmured. 'Do you think he's won them over?'

'I think he has certainly put doubts in their minds about rebelling,' Keph replied. 'I think Gadric still wants to go through with the rebellion, but I'm not too sure the others do. Talan seems only to want Jessa, and that would be easier for him to do via marriage than by rebelling. Borden and Locan seem more interested in the safety of the people of Bronze Keep than overthrowing the king. It might just have worked, but I wouldn't bet on anything just yet.'

'Have your people draw up an agreement,' Gadric said suddenly. 'I think I would like to consider it back in my quarters.'

'Very well,' said Cassien. 'I shall have it done immediately. I hope you will be as satisfied with the agreement as I am.'

The servants were summoned to remove the last plates and dishes from the table, whilst the nobles parted with civil, if slightly stiff, pleasantries. The whole artificiality of it was clear to see; Keph even heard some of the guards and servants remarking on it as he passed them on his way to and from the kitchens. Everybody knew that Cassien was playing a game with Gadric, but nobody was naive enough to think that it would last, or that it would pass without bloodshed. Keph could see from the looks on their faces that they were expecting something. But Keph knew from experience that whatever it was they were expecting, the reality would inevitably be more extreme.

Chapter 9.

Keph left the hall with the Bronze Keep delegation. Baron Gadric had been sceptical of his reassignment at first, but after Borden assured him Keph was a good servant and excellent cook, Gadric subsided.

They crossed the courtyard to the south wing, and Gadric went with his sons and grandson to his chambers to await the arrival of the agreement Cassien had promised. Keph, on the other hand, made his way to the kitchens. He did not stay there long though; as a servant and Segrata member he knew all the secret passages in every wing of the palace. He knew there was one that led to the master guest room, where the four nobles of Bronze Keep would be waiting for the trade agreement.

It was easy to disappear in the servants' passages in the palace, courtesy of the lack of light and the old stone foundations that created small chinks and alcoves in the walls. It took barely a moment for him to slip into one of these alcoves and move aside the tapestry that concealed the secret passage's entrance. He darted inside, arranged the tapestry neatly behind him and dashed through the narrow passages, up towards the second floor, slowing to a walk before he reached the end of the passage so as to get his breath back. To allow them to hear his heavy breathing through the wall would be a stupid mistake.

With his breath recovered and his heart beating normally, he approached the wall at the end of the passage. There was a small hole for him to put his eye to, through which he could see the whole of the room.

It was a fairly large room, with a four poster bed at the far end and a desk at the near one, along with a pair of comfortable but simple chairs. A small annex housed the washroom, and a dozen paintings and tapestries lined the walls. Gadric and Borden were sat in the chairs, with Locan stood leaning on the wall and Talan perched on the desk.

'Are you actually taking the king's proposal seriously, father?' asked Locan. 'Or are you playing him?'

'My gut tells me to stay with the original plan,' Gadric replied. 'But I know that if we do there will be a lot of blood spilled and the possibility of our being completely wiped out, though that was always the risk. Now, however, Cassien has outplayed us and given us something so materially beneficial we could profit from this and postpone the rebellion another year or even two. By then we could be so much more superior and have more allies. We could wage a proper war of rebellion instead of a coup inside the palace.'

'I think the king has more trade agreements than he's letting on,' Borden said. 'He's willing to give us all this for so little in return. He must have another way of making profits. And if he has any sense he will ensure he can make his position stronger through those agreements than ours will be after this one.'

'He knows what we're planning,' said Gadric. 'I could see it in his eyes. He knows why we're here in such force, why we're doing what we're doing, and he knows exactly how to make us stop and think and second guess ourselves. He's not intelligent. He's not a politician. He's cunning and deceitful and manipulative. He's got us right where he wants us.'

'Then we do something different,' Talan said. 'Something he won't expect us to do, and something we would not normally do.'

'Are you prepared to calculate yet another set of risks?' Locan pushed himself off the wall and locked his gaze with Talan's. 'We have spent so long working our way towards this rebellion, planning every little bit and calculating the risks over everything we do, and now we have more and more options being given to us. We can't have all of them, but each of them has a risk or a drawback of some kind.'

'I'm not giving this rebellion up so easily,' Gadric said. 'Not after everything we've done for it. I have been working towards this for twenty years, and I won't be stopped now. I'm not doing this for the title or the lands; I'm doing this for the people, because they deserve a better leader than Cassien.'

'You can't let your hatred get the better of you,' Borden said. 'We can't afford for anything to go wrong. Not now. Not when we're so close to achieving something.'

'Father's right,' agreed Talan. 'We've come so far, we have to get something out of this visit here. We have to get something positive to show for our troubles. I say we get the kingdom.'

'Talan – ' began Borden.

'That's why we came here in the first place, isn't it? To overthrow Cassien and take the throne? If we don't have anything to show for what we've done, we'll lose the support of the other nobles and be on our own again.'

'What about Jessa?' said Locan. 'You said yourself that you didn't deny her attractions, but do you think you can have both her and the kingdom if we rebel? Father, I know we are doing this for the people of Sorl, but we must think of our own people first – the people of Bronze Keep; the bandits are becoming bolder every day, especially with winter coming in soon, and if we sign this agreement it will ensure we can keep our people safe enough to allow us to move on Cassien much easier come this time next year.'

'I think we can use Jessa to our advantage, actually,' said Talan. 'I think she likes me, and she doesn't seem happy with her position. Give me a chance, and I think I can persuade her to help us. That way we have someone on the inside, and we can go through with our original plan. Besides, if we take over the throne, we can have the entirety of these trade agreements.'

'I agree,' said Gadric. 'Once you have Jessa on your side, we'll start the rebellion with her on the inside.'

A knock on the door announced the arrival of the agreement. Locan answered it, took the paper and handed it to Gadric, who immediately placed it face down on the desk and folded his arms.

'Jessa's quarters are in the east wing, not the north,' said Borden. 'Go this evening, persuade her to help, and then we strike in the morning.'

Keph moved back, further into the passage and away from the wall, his mind already working. It seemed clear that the first thing he should do was report directly to Fadrinar in the west wing, but there was always the risk of him being spotted leaving the guest quarters. After all, he was a servant; why should he need to go to the west wing?

No, reporting to Fadrinar was out of the question. Too dangerous.

If anything, the north wing was the only one to which he could credibly go without arousing too much suspicion. He could always come up with an alibi of some sort that would be believable enough. Not only that, but the king himself would be in the north wing, and his valet Nard was, of course, Segrata. If Keph could reach the north wing unopposed, he could get an immediate audience with Cassien and explain everything.

Yes. The north wing. He would report to the king directly.

He set off quickly, back through the secret passages to one that would bring him out near the kitchens. He emerged unhindered and used the side door to leave the wing. Not wanting to draw attention to himself, he slowed his pace for the walk to the north wing, and entered by another side door. Then he picked up the pace again, up the stairs and along the corridors until he reached the royal apartments. He practically ran into Nard as he turned the corner.

'I need to see the king immediately,' he said urgently, breathing hard. 'I can't afford to get to Fadrinar. This has to go to the king himself.'

Nard admitted him to Cassien's quarters without question, and the king turned quickly upon the sudden entry. Keph bowed and explained the conversation he had overheard between the rebels. Cassien listened closely. Then he said,

'I knew Jessa disliked me, but I had hoped this afternoon would show her why I need her with me. The sad thing about this business is that I know she would rather have her own independence than conform to what society expects from her, and indeed to what I expect of her. I have no doubts about her siding with Gadric and the rest of his rebels. Talan intends to make his move tonight, you say?'

'Yes, sire.'

'And then they launch their attack in the morning?'

'Yes, sire.'

'They can have the south wing,' the king said abruptly. 'I won't divert Ostion's men to it, otherwise the rebels will know we're onto them, and they'll change their plans. I want Gadric to be confident enough he will not alter his preparations. For that to happen, he has to control part of the palace, and I would be very surprised indeed if he does not start with the south wing.'

'What about Talan and Jessa?'

'If he wants her so much, he can have her. If I remove her to a place where she has no freedom, she will rebel of her own accord and we shall have to contend both with her and the rebels. Clearly, we cannot afford that. Once she does side with Gadric, I will order the men to bar her passage into any wing that we still control, but I do not want her killed. I still need her so that she can marry the man I want to be my successor, whoever he may be. Besides, she has spent most of her life confined to the east wing. True, she knows her way around the north wing, but I doubt she could be much help except as a guide through the corridors. She may be spirited, but she has never been adventurous. I wouldn't worry about it if I were you, Keph. Now that you have told me, I can have everything under control. For that I commend you.'

'Thank you, sire.'

'You're welcome. Now, once the fighting starts it will be dangerous for you to leave the rebels again. Indeed, you have taken a very great but ultimately necessary risk coming here now. Until the victory is safely ours, I do not want you to risk leaving them to bring either me or Fadrinar information. If you have a message to send, send it via courier bird. Fadrinar tells me every wing has some stashed away somewhere.'

'I will, sire. Thank you for hearing me out.'

'Thank you for bringing this to me. You are invaluable, Keph. Not only as a cook, but as a Segrata agent as well. Good luck.'

Keph's return to the south wing was at a slower pace now that there was no urgency. Out of courtesy he stopped by Deel's room. After all, if there was to be violence the next day, it was only fair to warn his friend in advance.

'Just to warn you,' he said, 'As of tomorrow, Baron Gadric and his men will be trying to take over the palace by force. The palace will become a battleground, so stay close to the king and don't go doing anything stupid. I know what you're like.'

'I would never do anything stupid, Keph. You know that!'

'Really? Words of love and adoration from a balcony? Perhaps you really have gone mad.'

'If ever I go truly mad I should think myself the luckiest of men. To have such freedom and openness of mind must be so exhilarating and so liberating! Oh to be free of the mortal coils that shackle my mind to this plane and restrain my genius. I would become the greatest mind in the world, without equal in every facet of life – '

Keph decided not to stay for the conclusion, closing the door quietly so as not to disturb Deel's mad, muffled ravings.

Chapter 10.

Dusk fell, and the servants made their masters' beds before both retired for the night. Some of the nobles stayed awake to read, to play at cards or dice, or to write. The gardeners packed up their tools and returned to their quarters, as did the cleaners. The stables were shut for the night and the horses locked safely inside. One by one, lamps went out.

Prince Talan, however, remained awake. He was unarmed and dressed in dark clothes. It was but a short walk from the south wing to the east wing, but he had decided to be sure that nobody saw him. The rebellion could not afford to take unnecessary risks or make unnecessary mistakes, especially now they were so close to success.

He set off once most of the lamps were extinguished from the east wing's windows. Fortunately, that of Lady Jessa was still on; he did not want to have to wake her and then try to persuade her to join the rebellion. He knew very little of decorum between men and women, but knew that doing something as serious and as important as trying to convince her to betray the king was not something that was to be attempted immediately after waking her up.

For a tall man he moved with feline silence, his long strides easily and quickly covering the open distance between the wings. It only then that it occurred to him he did not know the exact way to Jessa's room. It would be unadvisable to find someone who did know: that would make his intentions all too clear, and it would also make his presence known, which was exactly what he was trying to avoid.

The idea of climbing the vines on the outside of the wall and gaining entrance through the balcony briefly occurred to him, but he was wise enough to know that stunts like that only worked in plays. Perhaps he could use the balcony as a marker, make a mental note of which window it backed on to, and then use that as a reference point once inside so that he knew which room he was going for. But that always had the possibility for errors, which Gadric had expressly told him to avoid making.

His dilemma was concluded when footsteps on the balcony drew his attention. He looked up quickly and saw Jessa herself standing there, looking out towards the south wing. He needed no further opportunity, and called up quietly.

'Lady Jessa!'

She jumped, startled, and looked down. Upon seeing Talan she visibly relaxed and leaned over the edge towards him.

'What are you doing here so secretly?' she asked, a smile playing on her lips. Not having much experience with women, Talan found it hard to decide whether she was being polite or whether she was in some way toying with him. Either way, he had only one answer to give.

'I have to talk to you urgently. It cannot wait.'

'Climb up,' she whispered back. 'Don't risk the stairs.'

With relative ease he pulled himself up the ropes of ivy and over onto the balcony. Now that he stood next to her, he realised exactly how short she was compared to him. She led him inside and closed the doors to the balcony, then unlocked the door to the corridor and checked outside, before closing and locking it again. Then she turned to face him.

'What could bring a strong young man like you to my bedroom so late at night?'

'Honesty and openness,' Talan replied.

'I like an honest man,' she said. 'Is there nothing else I can do for you, my handsome prince?'

'Doing me this one favour will be enough, I think.'

'And what is this one favour?'

Talan hesitated, wondering how best to go about asking her to betray her uncle. Having had little success with tact in the past, he decided to be direct.

'You don't like your uncle, do you?' he asked.

'No,' she said sharply. 'I don't like him. I have been hoping to make it obvious to him ever since I learned how to dislike him.'

'But you like me?'

The sudden change in her was remarkable. From being so harsh and scathing of Cassien she turned alluring and enthralling.

'Intensely,' she replied. 'Did I make it obvious enough?'

'You did indeed. Did I reciprocate it clearly enough?'

'You do talk funny. Explain to me that word you used – reciprocate.' She tilted her head back and smiled, gazing up at him. 'It sounds so useful.'

'For a lady with access to such extensive libraries, you don't use them much,' he observed.

'Well why should I, when I can always have a man explain things for me? Now tell me . . . what does the word *reciprocate* mean?'

'To respond in kind,' he explained, trying to keep his distance for the moment, until he felt as comfortable as she clearly did.

'Ah! In that case, yes you did reciprocate it clearly enough. In fact, you could hardly have reciprocated it clearer.'

'In that case,' he said, taking a few steps backwards, 'I must ask that you do a very important thing, for me and my family, and indeed the kingdom.'

'Hmm,' she hummed. 'If you ask me to do a favour, it will be for you alone, young prince. I do not bestow my favour on so many people at once. Now tell me what you would have me do. Let me see if I can grant you your wish.'

'Your uncle is the king, but he is also a tyrant. You must have heard about his atrocities over the past years: he starved the village of Pelbrook so that his nobles had enough food for the winter. He allows the gutters to overflow with filth while the rich fill their pockets with gold. He raised the taxes in countless villages in order to pay for the construction of a new statue. Most of those villages suffered famines because he took more than double the previous tax.'

'I know what a tyrant my uncle is, Talan,' she said, turning abruptly hard and coarse again. 'I am not as ignorant as I seem, but what is there that can be done about him?'

Then she caught the gleam in Talan's eye.

'That's why you're here!' she gasped. 'You're not here to talk on behalf of the other nobles. Your grandfather is going to overthrow the king!'

'He is,' Talan said. 'And we . . . I . . . want your support. Will you join us? Will you help us?'

She stared into his eyes, long and hard, and then she said,

'You're taking an awful lot on faith. If I had refused, what would you have done then? You had told me a rebellion was about to happen. Would you let it go because of what you feel, or would you have killed a lady?'

'That's irrelevant,' he replied. 'I asked for your help because I knew you would not refuse to give it. I've seen and heard how much you dislike the king, and I would have to be blind and deaf not to notice your advances towards me. I knew you would not refuse.'

'My daring prince knows me well, it seems,' she said playfully, 'even though we have hardly got acquainted. If, for example, I was a selfish girl, what would I get out of this?'

'Once my grandfather takes control he can give the kingdom to you, and you would have a kingdom to rule and to mend. You would have the opportunity to atone for your uncle's mistakes. If you want him to keep control, you can hand your claim to him and have a free life at last.'

'And?' she prompted. 'What would you give me?'

'If I may be so bold,' he said, 'I would give you devotion and love for the rest of my life. You can depend on it . . . my lady.'

'Hmm,' she hummed again. 'You know exactly what a girl like me wants . . . my prince. I think,' she said, stepping closer, 'I accept your offer.' She leaned up and kissed him lightly on the cheek. 'I think your grandfather can have the throne,' she smiled. 'That way we can spend our time being . . . productive, perhaps producing a few heirs for you to pass the kingdom onto once it's yours. And I get to be queen anyway, regardless of who takes the throne. I think I have just accepted a very attractive offer, don't you?'

'I don't think I'm in as good a position as you to judge that.'

'However,' she said briskly, 'I can't help you if I'm stuck in here. I need the freedom to act, so once you have the south wing under your control, come and get me out of this one. Then I can help. Out of interest, exactly how do you see me helping? I can't fight or make grand plans. What can I do?'

'You can give us the information we need to make the rebellion progress quicker and easier,' he replied. 'Anything you know about the king's weaknesses, or the palace's weaknesses, or anything else you believe can help us.'

'I think I can do that,' she said. 'You can depend on it; once you set me free, the Segrata will cease to be a problem.'

Chapter 11.

Keph awoke the next morning with a sick feeling in his stomach. He had always trusted his instincts, and they told him that this morning would be the start of a few long, bloody days. There was no doubting Gadric's intention to seize the south wing in the morning, before the king's forces could react, and from there proceed to one of the others. Keph knew that he would be caught up right in the middle of it all, wanting to help the king but confined to his role as a servant to Prince Borden. He desperately wanted to be open about his defiance of Gadric and his rebellious schemes, but knew that doing so would jeopardise his position as the inside man in Gadric's rebellion.

But once the fighting started, Keph would not be near it; why should a servant be anywhere near the fighting, especially a servant who was known to be one of Cassien's most valued?

A sudden, horrible thought struck him.

What if they decide they can't take the risk? What if they decide I'm too unsafe to have around?

There was a knock on the door, and a voice filtered through the keyhole.

'Keph! It's Prince Borden. Get dressed and come out. I'll be waiting.'

Certain it was because they distrusted him, Keph took his time in doing as Borden had commanded so that he could have as much time as possible to think and to improvise. But nothing occurred to him by the time he finally opened the door, unable to put it off any longer, and he stepped out into the corridor to find Borden standing waiting.

The prince was wearing armour and carrying his weapons. A mail shirt covered his stout frame, and a domed, open-faced helm was tucked under his arm. At his hip were a wide-bladed sword and a small knife, and a crossbow was slung on his back.

'Good morning, Keph,' he said sternly. 'Come with me.'

Without waiting, he set off down the corridor and started to make his way up towards the upper floors of the wing. All around them, the soldiers of Gadric's retinue were donning armour, sharpening swords and sighting down crossbows. It was clear enough that they were preparing for a fight, and though to most of the servants it came as a shock that the soldiers were gearing up, to Keph it was precisely as he had expected.

Borden led the way up to Gadric's quarters, knocked and entered.

It was as it had been when Keph had looked through the spy hole the previous day, with Gadric in the same chair, Locan back leaning on the wall and Talan once again perched on the desk. Borden remained by the door as Keph was ushered into the middle of the room to face Gadric.

'I think it strange,' the baron said, 'that the king should give my son his most valued servant the very day before we start to overthrow him. Why are you here, again? Did you request the post, or does the king have another reason for placing you with us?'

'As far as I am aware,' Keph replied, wary of not implicating himself, 'the king assigned me to your son because he felt it a gesture of respect to give his guests the use of one of his best servants.'

'You have seen by now that we are preparing to fight the king and his men,' Gadric continued. 'You were not previously aware of this?'

'No, sir. I wasn't.'

'Was the king?'

'I do not know the king as well as he seems to know me. I cannot answer that question with any certainty.'

Gadric was silent for a few seconds before continuing.

'For a servant, you speak quite eloquently.'

'One of my friends is Deel the playwright,' Keph explained. 'He and I often pick up phrases from one another. And it also comes from being so continuously in the presence of the king and his nobles. It is not as hard as it seems to imitate their eloquence and sophistication.'

'Hmm,' the baron said doubtfully. 'You also seem to know how to use them properly. Most remarkable for someone of your social inferiority. So now I have a problem. I am going to take over this wing of the palace in a few moments. What few guards the king has here will be defeated, and the servants will not dare to fight back against us. But you are in the service of my son, and I am not inclined to trust you. What if you take it upon yourself to try and stop my liberation of this kingdom? What do I do about you?'

Again, he was silent. Then he leaned forwards in his chair and stared Keph in the eye. Keph did his best to keep his own expression neutral and unassuming in the face of Gadric's furrowed brow and stern, dark gaze.

'But why?' the baron asked quietly. 'Why are you here? What is the king playing at, giving you to me? I do not believe that he is so ignorant as to believe we are actually willing to talk and make peace with him. All this talk about restoring relations between us is a farce! He knows it can never happen, and yet he accepts us here all the same, doesn't question the number of men I bring with me, and makes no effort to have me watched. At least, not openly. That, I believe, is where you come in, Keph. I think that you are spying on me for the king. What do you say to that?'

'I would say that you are entitled to your opinion, and in your position I can see it would make sense. But it is also a bold claim, sir, to expect me to be able to spy on you when I am in fact in the service and company of your son.'

Keph watched his words take effect as Gadric's eyes narrowed in suspicion and scrutiny. It seemed the only hope he had of preserving his position was to talk his way out of suspicion by outwitting Gadric. Considering how stubborn the baron was, Keph resigned himself to a long, dangerous and careful interview.

'If you really are a spy for the king,' Gadric said, 'you are playing a dangerous and yet clever game. It may surprise you to hear that I am a fair man, and I don't punish without cause like the king does. But I do know when it is better to be safe than sorry. I have no proof that you are Cassien's spy, but I cannot allow you to walk free while the prospect is still possible, and yet I do not want to punish or accuse you wrongly.'

'May I suggest,' said Borden, 'that he stays with me and my men. You said yourself that I will probably be doing the least fighting over the course of this liberation, and I can spare a few men to make sure Keph doesn't do anything against us.'

'If he does though, are you willing enough to take the responsibility for what happens?' asked Locan.

'I am,' said Borden. 'I have faith both in Keph's common sense, and in his sense of self-preservation. I think he would decide it unwise to make a move when so obviously watched and guarded. Besides, if he is not a spy, he will be safe enough to satisfy any curiosity he may have and see exactly what is happening.'

'If you're willing to take responsibility for him, then take him,' Gadric said, leaning back. 'I don't want to have to worry about him as well as the rebellion. He's your problem now, Borden.'

Keph looked round at the prince, but received a blank gaze in return.

'Now that's settled,' said Gadric, 'I think it's time to start this rebellion and liberate the kingdom. You know what you're doing. When we've secured this wing, we give the men a small rest and then march on the east wing.'

Keph went with Borden's group of five hundred men to secure the upper floors of the wing. They opened every door and cleared every room of servants or guards, capturing who they could but killing those who attempted to fight back. Borden led from the front, with Keph by his side, unarmed and unarmoured.

They reached the gallery on the third floor and waited while the soldiers worked their way along, searching every room thoroughly. Keph looked again at Borden, and saw that the prince's face was as cold and hard as his father's. Borden must have felt him looking, and said,

'I hope you don't make me regret taking you with me like this. But we can't take any chances and I don't want a potential spy anywhere near my father. My men and I are the reserves, so you're staying well out of the fighting with us.'

'Do you think I'm a spy?'

'It's possible, but my father is right: it would make us too much like the king if we were to judge you without evidence one way or another. And the king is exactly what we're fighting against.'

'Rich words coming from someone who has had almost twenty innocents killed already.'

Borden rounded on him.

'Innocents? Those guards who fought back were not innocent. They are with the king, and the king is corrupted by his own power. I wish we didn't have to fight like this. I wish we could settle all this peacefully, but the king will never accept the signing of some piece of paper. To settle anything with the king one must be forceful, brutal even, and stand up to him. Doing that includes killing his men. But you have failed to notice that we only kill the ones who resist. Yes, we have killed, and there will be much more killing before this liberation is over, but we are not like the king. These killings are not cold or cruel or brutal. They are necessary, Keph. They are a necessity that must be taken if we are to secure this kingdom as a better place for future generations.

There was very little that Keph could say in reply to this. Fortunately, he did not have to think of a response, as the soldiers reported that the gallery had been cleared. From there they moved along the corridors and passages in a sweeping action, sparing no room or alcove from their search. Slowly, the group of prisoners grew larger, as did the number of corpses. As the guards saw more and more of their comrades imprisoned, they fought back harder, refusing to be taken prisoner like their fellows.

Keph counted how many died at the hands of Borden's men: twelve servants and thirty three guards. The prisoners, by the time the upper floors were cleared, numbered almost seventy.

They were brought down into the main hall and placed with those captured by Locan, Talan and Gadric in other sections of the wing, bringing the total number of prisoners up to just over two hundred.

With the wing secure and the assurance from Locan that nobody had escaped to take word to the king, Gadric ordered the prisoners locked in the main hall with access to food and water, before announcing the attack on the east wing.

The attack was launched with speed and precision. Gadric and Talan led their men towards the front door, while Locan led his to a side door. Borden remained at the rear of the attack to act as a reserve force in the event of a counter attack from one of the other wings of the palace.

The front door was quickly broken down from the sheer number of men who threw their weight against it, including Talan, and he and Gadric headed the main assault. Locan broke in the side door with relative ease and pressed the attack from there.

It seemed that even though Cassien had told Keph he was going to offer no resistance to the rebels' attack on the east wing, he had placed enough guards there to cause the attack a bit of trouble. There was no officer or commanding presence among the defenders, who numbered significantly less than the baron's forces, but they were well disciplined all the same. Of the three hundred defenders, all were killed, but they took with them nearly five hundred – a full quarter – of the rebels, through a better knowledge of the wing's passages than Gadric's men. The sheer aggression and disregard for their own safety, as well as a refusal to give ground, made Keph think that they had been ordered to fight to the death.

Of the twelve hundred palace guard, a quarter were now dead. But so was a quarter of the rebels' force. There were some commanders who would consider it a loss to lose even the same as the enemy. Other commanders would call it brutal, but also an ultimately necessary sacrifice.

It did not take a lot of imagination to know which of these things King Cassien would say.

The east wing was taken, giving the rebels control of half the palace in the space of a morning, and Lady Jessa was freed and welcomed into Gadric's inner circle with grace and gratitude. Borden dismissed Keph and his soldiers, ordering that the servant be kept under guard at all times.

Keph's guard was a tall, broad, deep-voiced soldier called Drogan. Though underneath his weather-beaten and scarred face he was a young man, he had the look of an aged veteran. Considering Keph was supposed to be being kept under guard, Drogan was strangely conversational. At Keph's observation of this, the soldier replied,

'What else is there to do? My sword's still sharp; no point sharpening it. My armour's still shining; no point buffing it anymore. You get so used to having things to do when you're a soldier, you forget how to sit and do nothing. It's a shame: the times I'll be doing things and stopping being bored is when I'm told to kill people. To be honest, I'd rather be bored than kill servants though.'

'You don't agree with what the baron is doing then?'

'I understand what he's trying to achieve, and I admire his courage and determination for going through with it, but I don't agree with the violence of it all. If the king was more willing to talk, we might be tempted to talk as well, but the king wants to deal with everything through force and violence. The only way to deal with that is to respond in kind. Violence is the only language King Cassien understands.'

'There's something about this that *I* don't understand,' said Keph. 'People keep talking about atrocities the king has committed, but I don't ever remember hearing about any.'

'Did you hear about the village of Pelbrook last year?' said Drogan.

'I heard that their harvest had produced the surplus required to supplement the poor harvest around the city itself.'

'Lies,' the soldier spat. 'The king took what the villagers needed in order to feed his own court. Half the village starved to death after that. And what about the Mithar incident? What did you hear about that?'

'The town wouldn't allow the king's men to search it for a fugitive, so he had half a dozen men killed to stress the urgency of the situation, so that they would obey him.'

'It was worse than that! He didn't even offer them the chance to allow his men in peacefully – he thought the fugitive was too dangerous to take any risks against, so he slaughtered half the village to be sure. And he may not have even killed the fugitive; the man he was after could have survived and be walking free. Tell me how your great king can justify all that.'

'There is nothing that can justify that,' Keph said, slightly perplexed, 'but I cannot believe that the king would slaughter people out of hand. I know he is a strict ruler and a disciplinarian, but I doubt he would really allow that many to die without cause. He has made bad decisions sometimes, and he even admits it himself, but – '

'The king is a monster,' Drogan interrupted bitterly. 'I fail to see how that makes him a good king. Who knows the true extent of what he's done? Nobody wants to know, or even imagine! This is why he has to die.'

Even so, Keph was not convinced. He knew that if he said anything Drogan would become even more angry, and such was the precariousness of Keph's position, he did not want his guard taking a thorough dislike to him. So he kept quiet and tried to make sense of it all.

It was clear enough that there was a deception of some kind going on, but whether it was by the king to his people or Gadric to his men was a different matter entirely. If Cassien had been deceiving his people, it was not so unacceptable as Drogan was making out, was it? He had the authority to do whatever he deemed best, so why should he be questioned, most of all why should he be questioned by his servant and member of the Segrata? The relationship between the king and the Segrata was one of mutual trust and respect. Why should the king betray his subjects' trust in such an underhand manner?

And yet on the other side it was a similar question: why should Gadric deceive *his* subjects with such outrageous and aggressive accusations against the king? The only answer that seemed plausible was that he wanted the power of kingship for himself and his family, so that he could rule in his own brutal way. It was, after all, a brutal act he was performing. He talked of *liberating the kingdom*, but as far as Keph could see the kingdom did not need to be liberated, least of all from Cassien: he was a competent ruler who prevented his people being harmed by outside influences, and he made the treasury prosper though solid trade agreements. He had proven that in his trade agreement with the Dashaar.

Keph could see that Gadric was misguided in some way if he thought that a flourishing kingdom like Sorl needed a new leadership. The king had said himself that he intended to turn Sorl into the envy of all the other kingdoms this side of the Jade Peaks. How better could that be done than with a strong leader who knew how to get exactly what he wanted, and who had firm control of his people and his ministers?

But even rationalising it like that, the flaw was that the king did not have control of everyone; Bronze Keep still believed that he was in the wrong, and intended to prevent him strengthening Sorl. Not only that, but it seemed that there were other families among the Sorlian nobility who had formed similar opinions to Gadric – Duke Cardil was a prominent member of the dissidents, as was Count Seldin. Both held a lot of influence in the kingdom.

That was always the problem with leaders like Gadric and Cassien: they were able to influence the right people to get what they wanted. In many cases it was for the good of the kingdom and the people, but leaders like Gadric abused their power, used it for selfish reasons, used it to gain even more power. Gadric was leading a rebellion because now that he had gained the support of other nobles and had them under his thumb he could not bear the thought of losing them. And the only way to do that was to ensure that he had enough power centred on himself that they would never defy him again.

He sought more power because he feared to lose what power he already had.

And Cassien ruled with a strong arm because he feared for the fate of his kingdom if a ruthless monster like Gadric took control.

One way or another, regardless of the outcome of the rebellion, the king of Sorl would be motivated by fear, and would therefore rule through fear.

Chapter 12.

After securing the east wing, word was circulated throughout the soldiers that they would be moving next on the west wing, to eliminate the palace guard headquarters and armouries. However, the men needed a rest, and were told that no further progress would be made until the Segrata influence had been neutralised.

Keph received this news with dread. Surely the first Segrata target to be eliminated would be Commissar Fadrinar. But the king had expressly said that Keph was not to leave the rebels' camp for any reason. He considered attempting to send a message via courier bird, as per the king's suggestion, but Drogan had been ordered to follow Keph everywhere he went to make sure he didn't try anything, as Gadric put it, *foolish enough to make me angry.*

It seemed there was no way to reach Fadrinar and warn him except by taking the risk and going himself. But that would be certain to expose him as a Segrata agent, and he would no longer be able to work from inside the rebels. It would also mean that he was disobeying a direct order from the king. There was very little that he could do to harm the rebels in any case, considering he was effectively a prisoner.

He had, therefore, only two choices. The first would be to stay where he was and watch as the rebellion happened, unable to do anything to help his king. The second would be to orchestrate an escape from the rebels, thereby revealing his nature as a spy, and warn Fadrinar of the impending attack on the Segrata.

He had no difficulty in deciding. But the problems he now faced were how to escape and how to work out what form the attack on the Segrata would take, as well as trying to predict when it would happen.

It seemed logical that Fadrinar would be the first target: cut off the head and the body collapses. Fadrinar would, most likely, be in the west wing for most of the day, coordinating the Segrata, and therefore hard to get to. It had already been decided that the rebels were not going to attack the west wing until the next day, so the attempt to get to Fadrinar would have to be either an individual or a small group. It would be impossible for them to enter the wing during the day without being seen, so the only other time would be once night fell. That meant that Keph had the remainder of the day to plan and carry out his escape.

Even so, he did not want to have to wait long, however necessary it might be.

He spent the remainder of the morning trying to work out what sort of opportunity would be the easiest and most efficient to create. After all, the opportunity was never going to spontaneously present itself. But his thinking process was constantly slowed and distracted by Drogan, who seemed to want nothing except to talk. In the brief moments of silence, Keph's brain worked frantically, searching for anything that would give him any idea of what sort of opportunity he could create.

Perhaps that was Drogan's design in talking to him: to distract him from making any sort of progress in planning an escape. It was either that or Drogan was preventing boredom again. Either way, it took all of Keph's awareness and willpower to plan and talk at the same time. He had never before realised how tiring planning an escape and trying to maintain a cover could be, and privately hoped he never had to do it again.

By mid afternoon, however, he had finally found a solution. The frustrating part of it was that he could not implement his plan until nearly sundown, by which time the person or persons sent to eliminate Fadrinar could well be on their way to him. It also meant that he would only get the one attempt.

The time came towards late afternoon, as the light was fading and the sun setting, and Keph was quick to put his plan into action. Drogan spent much of his time fiddling with his whetstone while he talked, and Keph had observed that it was engraved with a small 'D' to mark is as his. On the most recent occasion of its being put away, Keph had slipped it out of the soldier's pocket and hidden it in his own sleeve. This was the first part of his plan.

The second part was as a result of the lack of men caused by Cassien's deployment of the guardsmen in the east wing. To properly defend the wing, some who would normally have been exempt from patrolling were required to do so. This included Drogan, whose patrol of the upper floors, along with another soldier, was due to start at five o'clock. Though he had offered Keph to remain with another soldier in the main area of the wing, Keph had declined, saying that he quite preferred Drogan's company and would rather not be given a guard he didn't know. Drogan had nodded and replied with a simple,

'Fair enough.'

The two of them set off for the upper floors, picking up the second soldier on the way. Keph was familiar with the secret passages, and was ready when his opportunity came to implement the final stage of his plan.

Walking with Drogan, slightly behind the other soldier, he let the whetstone drop from his sleeve and into the palm of his hand, before flicking his wrist discreetly and allowing the stone to skim quickly past the front soldier and land in the corridor ahead. At the clatter of stone on wood, the soldier in front started forwards to investigate. He picked it up and looked at it, then turned to Drogan and said,

'Isn't this yours, Drogan?'

Drogan strode over to have a look, and Keph stepped smartly into a nearby alcove, pushing on the wall to open the secret door. It swung in quietly, and Keph receded into the passage beyond. He shut the door behind him, but didn't wait to see if he could hear the soldiers' reaction to his sudden disappearance, knowing that the moment his disappearance was noticed, the alarm would be raised and guards would be searching for him. He was determined to have left the wing before the search could get fully underway.

He dashed through the passages until he reached one that ran in a spiral down through the wing. From what he could remember, he believed it to be on the inside of the huge central pillar in the library. Upon reaching the bottom he ran through a series of well memorised twists and turns until he came to the exit he was looking for. It brought him out into the corridor outside the kitchens, at the end of which was the side door to the wing. Without waiting to see if he had been spotted, he darted to the door and opened it, being sure to close it once he had passed through.

It was a short run across the courtyard to the west wing, and he had no doubt that he had been seen from the windows of the east wing – it would have taken a blind person not to see him sprinting across the courtyard. But he was too far away now for them to do anything about him, and he kept running until he reached the main entrance of the west wing. Even in the dusk the guards recognised him and let him through.

He hurried through the wing, not to the Segrata meeting place, but to Fadrinar's own office at the back of the first floor. He knocked quickly and was commanded to enter.

The office was small but well furnished, with an expensive cabinet, glass-fronted and wooden-backed, backing onto the wall behind a sleek oak desk with ornate carvings on its legs. Around the walls hung half a dozen tapestries, each one depicting a lion in various stages of stalking, pouncing or chasing prey. Fadrinar liked to think that these pictures represented his agents. Keph thought it was inappropriate to view people like animals, or even to view animals as people. It was a clear enough distinction to make. But then, Fadrinar always had been one for abstract thinking. It was one of the reasons why he was commissar instead of someone else.

He was sat behind the desk, looking at the doorway expectantly. Upon seeing Keph his eyes narrowed.

'I thought you were infiltrating the rebels,' he said, leaning back in his chair. 'On the king's orders.'

'I was, sir,' Keph explained, 'but they became suspicious and rounded up all the servants to make sure none of them were spies. Naturally, they included me.'

'But you have escaped and come running to me. You have urgent news?'

'I do, sir.'

'Than let's have it.'

'The rebels will attack this wing first thing in the morning, but this evening they intend to eliminate the Segrata. I fear that they will start with you, sir. It seems the most logical thing to do.'

'Indeed,' said Fadrinar, his stern face showing no change as his brain processed this news. 'And I do not doubt the efficiency of the rebels. The baron is a great strategist; if he says the Segrata will no longer be a problem by tomorrow morning, then he has a way of making that happen. I appreciate the warning, Keph, but do you know how Gadric intends to eliminate us?'

'No I don't. I was unable to find that out.'

'Well, it can't be helped. I would have considered us fortunate indeed, in fact, if you had found out. But not to worry – we can at least be alert so that when the time comes, we are as ready as we can be. Now, there is one last thing you must do. You cannot go back to the rebels now, though I suppose you knew that already. Just in case I don't make it through until the morning, I am going to write an order for Commander Ostion. You will deliver it for me.'

Without hesitation he pulled a sheet of paper towards him and began to write.

'Don't bother trying to read it,' he murmured without looking up. 'It's written in an old code the commander taught me way back, for use when we had to make sure things stayed secret even from people we trusted. This is something I do not want the king getting hold of.'

He finished writing, pulled a small key out of his pocket, put it in the middle of the message and folded the paper up, sealing it with a wax imprint from his ring. The lion-shaped seal of the Segrata was familiar to Keph, but the way that Fadrinar had talked about the message made the insignia somehow different, almost foreign, as though Keph had never really known what it meant or stood for.

'When do I give this to the commander?' he asked.

'At a very specific time,' Fadrinar replied. 'Once the attack on this wing begins, give it enough time to get into full flow. Then take this to Ostion. He is not a subtle commander, and if he were to have it before the attack he would make his plans around it and the rebels would see something was up. They must believe things are going as planned for this to work.'

'I understand, sir,' said Keph, reaching out to take the message. But Fadrinar placed his hand over it quickly.

'No you don't, Keph,' he whispered. 'This message could turn the battle, and it's safe delivery to the commander is therefore paramount to our success. This message must get to Ostion, regardless of the cost to yourself or to anyone else. This is crucial to the king's survival, but he will hate Ostion and me when he finds out what I have sanctioned the commander to do. He might even execute us for it. He will find out when it happens – in fact I dare him to miss it – but I would rather he did not find out beforehand, otherwise he will put a stop to it. This message is all that matters to you from now on. Nothing else must matter to you . . . not yourself, not your brother, not even the king. Now do you understand?'

'I believe I do, sir.'

'Thank you, Keph,' Fadrinar said, releasing his hold on the message. Keph tucked it into his pocket.

Footsteps sounded outside the door. Fadrinar straightened attentively in his chair, and Keph strained his ears to listen.

'One person,' Fadrinar breathed. 'Fairly light, judging from the sound of the footsteps, and cautious judging by their frequency. But also determined.' He looked across at Keph. 'I think our assassin has arrived.'

Keph moved towards the wall, where Fadrinar kept his array of knives and swords.

'No, Keph,' the commissar hissed. 'You have to get away with that message. Immediately. There's a passage behind that cabinet.' He indicated the empty glass-faced cabinet behind his desk. 'It goes down to the meeting chamber. Don't risk going anywhere else tonight.'

'What about you, sir?' Keph hissed back.

There was a knock at the door.

'I'll stay,' Fadrinar whispered quickly. 'If they don't find me they'll turn this place upside down, and they'll find you and the message. That mustn't happen. Now go! And don't forget what I said.'

The commissar stood up and pushed Keph roughly into the secret passage behind the cabinet. As it closed, Keph stuck the toe of his boot in the gap so that it was practically closed, but he still had a crack to see and hear through.

The knock sounded again, and Fadrinar pulled a short sword from the rack on the wall. Then he opened the door and stepped back, allowing the assassin to enter.

Through the open door came Lady Jessa. She was dressed now in a mail shirt, like Gadric's soldiers, and wielded a short sword similar to

Fadrinar's. She walked to the middle of the room and allowed Fadrinar to close the door behind her.

'I wondered who they would send,' he said. 'I expected one of the princes to take on the role, not you. In fact, I didn't know for certain you had joined them.'

'Didn't know for certain?' she repeated. 'But you suspected?'

'I had seen your behaviour to the young prince, and I had seen his to you. It doesn't take a great leap of the imagination to suspect what his intentions were, and how easily you would be persuaded to take the opportunity provided to you. But I'm afraid you disappoint me, my lady.'

'Oh?' she said, raising her eyebrows. 'And how have I disappointed the great Commissar of the Segrata?'

'By disrespecting your uncle so much. I know that he has made a number of bad decisions, but everything he has been doing, he has been doing to make Sorl the best place it can be for when you succeed him. He wants you to inherit a strong kingdom that knows its place in the world and can assert it with pride and without fear of conflict.'

She laughed contemptuously.

'Don't try to put me off my task with all this talk of him doting on me. He has no respect for anyone but himself.'

'He adores you, my lady,' Fadrinar said. 'So much so that he put you somewhere he would not have to see your hatred for him.'

'What happens,' she asked, ignoring him completely, 'when you die? Does the famed and feared Segrata strike back? Or does it fall apart without the lion to lead it?'

'Every lion has his pride,' Fadrinar answered. 'And my agents are mine. Without me they will do what they have been ordered to do without fear, compassion or question. Killing the lion will not kill his pride.'

'That is one of the most abstract retorts I've heard in a long time,' she smiled. But it was a smile that spoke of arrogance and disdain. 'It isn't going to help you.'

She swung the sword towards him, and he blocked it neatly, pushing it away and stepping close for the counter thrust. She stepped back, and Keph saw her slip something from the belt of the mail shirt. In a deft sidestep she circled to Fadrinar's unguarded side and stabbed a small dagger into his side, burying it up to the hilt.

She pulled it out and stabbed again, then stepped away and let Fadrinar drop to his knees. The sword clattered out of his hand and clanged onto the floor, and his face contorted into a stunned kind of grimace. But Jessa had one more strike to make. She positioned herself behind the fallen commissar, the knife to one side of his throat, and gently drew it across.

Being careful not to get any of Fadrinar's blood on her armour or on the dress underneath, she walked quickly to the door and left the room, closing it softly behind her. Fadrinar's corpse slowly bled out onto the floor in her wake.

In the secret passage, Keph breathed out, looked away, and let the concealed door finally slide closed.

Chapter 13.

Keph spent an uncomfortable night in the Segrata meeting room. He didn't dare go back to his own quarters in the north wing, and to go anywhere out of the secret passages or the Segrata room was dangerous enough with Jessa potentially roaming around, searching for other agents.

He had not thought about it immediately, but he wondered now how she had got into the west wing. Cassien had said that he would order the guars to bar her entry, and there were guards on every door. He supposed she could have climbed in through one of the windows, but they were all shut and locked at night, which meant she would have had to have been a very skilled burglar to enter that way, and then know the guards' patrols inside out to avoid being spotted. Not only that, but a dress was an impractical thing to wear if trying to enter through a window. Even Keph could see that.

The only way someone could get into any wing of the palace undetected at night was if there was a secret entrance of some sort from one wing to another. In all his time as a Segrata agent Keph had never heard of any such passage, or found any record of one. But then, he had only been taught what Fadrinar knew, and neither of them had considered the fact there could be more.

And Jessa was the one who had had the wing containing the libraries all to herself for years; it looked like she had been using her time wisely. Indeed, more wisely than anyone gave her credit for.

Keph was woken in the morning by Nard, the king's valet.

'Good morning, Keph,' he said, observing him curiously. 'What are you doing down here?'

'Hiding,' Keph replied, trying to get some feeling back in his limbs. 'From Lady Jessa.'

'Lady Jessa? What for? The king says she is being held captive in the east wing.'

'The king is saying that so that his guards will recapture her alive,' Keph said. 'She has actually decided to join the rebels. She came here last night and killed the commissar.'

Nard's jaw dropped slowly as he comprehended the implication of Keph's words.

'The commissar? Dead?'

'I saw it myself. She stabbed him twice and then cut his throat.'

'By all the Gods!' breathed Nard. 'She is ruthless. But what about you?' he asked quickly. 'Are you alright?'

'I'm fine. I escaped into a secret passage before she arrived. But what are you doing down here, Nard?'

'Fadrinar said he wanted to meet Jerl and I this morning, in here. But I suppose that won't be happening now.'

'No, I suppose it won't.'

They turned suddenly at the sound of heavy footsteps, but relaxed when Jerl entered. His shoulders slouched a little and his eyes looked bleary.

'You look tired, little brother,' Keph remarked. 'What have you been up to?'

'I couldn't sleep,' Jerl said. 'Never can when I know they're coming for us the next morning. Don't worry about me though, Keph. Once things get underway I'll be right as rain again. There's nothing like a bit of adrenaline to wake you up.'

He looked round anxiously.

'Where's Fadrinar?'

'Dead,' Nard replied. 'Keph saw it yesterday evening.'

'It was Jessa,' Keph added. 'She has joined the rebels now, it seems.'

Jerl's eyes dropped.

'So what do we do?' he asked.

'We fight the rebels with everything we've got,' Keph replied. 'Before he died, Fadrinar gave me this.' He pulled the sealed message out of his pocket. 'Once the battle for this wing gets underway, I have to deliver this to Commander Ostion, no matter the cost. Fadrinar said it would ensure we have the advantage, but I don't know how, and he's written it in a code only he and Ostion know.' He looked meaningfully at Nard. 'Even the king is not to know.'

'Can we afford to let this go past the king?' Nard said.

'That depends on whether you trust Fadrinar and Ostion or not.'

'We're short on people to trust as it is,' said Jerl. 'If it will give us an advantage I'm willing to go behind the king's back.'

'As long as we don't go so far behind his back he classes us as rebels too,' said Nard. 'I suppose we have little choice. Fadrinar was Commissar for a reason. He knew what he was doing. Alright. You two do what you have to do. I'll report back to the king, get out of here before the fighting starts.'

'You do that,' agreed Keph. 'And make sure you look after him. Don't let him do anything rash. The rebels can't afford to make any mistakes now, and neither can we.'

'Agreed,' said Nard. 'Good luck. And if things don't work, I consider myself privileged to have known you two. I doubt Fadrinar could have asked for two more reliable agents.'

'If you're dishing out compliments, save some for yourself,' said Jerl. 'I think you need them more than we do – you have to work with the king every day.'

'Fair point.' Nard smiled. 'Good luck, gentlemen.'

The valet left the room, leaving Keph and Jerl in a resolute silence. Jerl moved to the door and put his hand on the handle.

'Stick with me,' Jerl said. 'Commander Ostion has given me command of the main door into the wing. He'll be coordinating from the window of the floor above via a series of runners. I think he wants to see how I command a large number of men. I'll make sure you get the space to run that message.'

'Alright,' said Keph. 'Just make sure you keep yourself safe too. I can't look out for you all the time.'

'Hey, who's the soldier?' Jerl said. 'I'm the one keeping you safe, remember?'

Keph nodded, only slightly reassured by his brother's ease and confidence.

'What time is it?' he asked, suddenly aware of the lack of clocks in the room.

'It was about eight o'clock when I came down,' Jerl replied. 'So perhaps about five past now. I imagine the rebels will be attacking again soon, and I want to be there to welcome them when they do. Besides, the men will need their leader with them sooner rather than later.'

Jerl led the way up the tight spiral stairs to the landing with the door to the rest of the palace. The stairs that led even further upwards were still blocked by the door to which only Fadrinar had had the key.

'I wonder what Fadrinar kept up there,' said Jerl. 'If anything was kept up there at all.'

'Fadrinar put a key inside the message for Ostion,' said Keph. 'I wonder if it was the key for this door.'

'Let's hope everything works so we can find out,' Jerl said, opening the door to the rest of the wing. 'Come on, Keph.'

At the end of the corridor they came to the main entrance hall into the wing. Around seven hundred soldiers guarded it, arrayed in their own companies and ranks, all of them facing the main door. The remaining two hundred, it seemed, were upstairs with Commander Ostion. A soldier from the closest detachment hurried up to Jerl.

'Sir,' he said crisply, saluting with sharp precision. 'The rebels are on the move already. Estimated a full one thousand men are moving on the main door, with a reserve of five hundred remaining in the courtyard.'

'Thank you,' said Jerl. 'Which of the rebel leaders is heading the main force?'

'Baron Gadric and Prince Talan, sir. Princes Locan and Borden are with the reserves.'

'There must be a reason for not committing Locan,' said Keph. 'Borden is the reserves commander, but I would have expected Locan to be in the thick of things.'

'So would I,' Jerl agreed. He turned to the soldier. 'Run to Commander Ostion and recommend that he watches the enemy reserves and has a contingency in place for when they make their move.'

'Yes, sir!'

The soldier set off up the stairs at a run.

'Those stairs are going to cause trouble,' Jerl said. 'They're right next to the main door. The moment the rebels break through they'll be in control of them.'

'Can't you defend the doorway itself?'

'Not with these men. They would need to be good, solid soldiers to hold a line like that against superior numbers. Besides, they've been trained to fight in space, with a bit of open ground to manoeuvre in. They wouldn't hold out long in that doorway. I'm keeping them back a bit to give them that space, even if it does mean giving the rebels space of their own.

'Now you stay well back, too,' he said. 'I'll let you judge when the time is right. Just send me a message and I'll force a gap open for you. I can't hold it open forever though; I'll have to pull back eventually, so when you go through, make it count. Once you're through I can pull the men back into a tighter formation, so don't keep us waiting.'

'I won't,' Keph said. 'Now go on, little brother. Give those men their leader.'

Jerl moved to the front company, drew his sword, and turned to face his men. Keph retired to behind the back company, suddenly aware of how exposed he felt with the urgent message in his pocket and only himself to rely on to deliver it safely.

'The rebels are on their way!' Jerl shouted. 'They outnumber us. You know we're not as well trained or equipped as they are, but we have something to fight for that they don't: a king and his kingdom! If we go down, so will the king, and so will Sorl. That's all there is to this, and I don't do speeches; so draw your swords, raise your shields, and prepare to defend your kingdom!' He turned and faced the door. 'Let them come!' he roared.

The echoed roar from the soldiers drowned out the first few charges the rebels made against the doors, but they soon broke in and spilled into the wing. Gadric and Talan charged at their head, barrelling into the defenders. The loyalist soldiers held their ground against the rush, and then began to fight back. Jerl fought at the front, keeping the line together with both his huge voice and his skilled sword arm. But with two leaders to look to the rebels began to gain the upper hand.

Despite his age, Gadric was still a capable warrior, and held his own with ease against two opponents. And Talan, though still young, showed great skill and maturity as a soldier, heading a small group that started to work its way into one side of the loyalist defence, splitting it open. Immediately the company in front of Keph rushed forwards to fill the gap, and Talan's men were repelled. The prince himself remained unscathed.

And between Keph and the staircase stood both the loyalists and the rebels, every single one of them caught up in the huge swirling melee.

Keph watched with trepidation as he tried to judge the best time to tell Jerl to make the gap. On the loyalists' left, Talan was still fighting to punch through, and on the right Gadric's line was holding steady. Jerl stood at the centre of it all, swinging and slicing with a fury bordering on savagery.

Half a dozen men emerged from the chaos and staggered back towards Keph, all of them wounded to some degree. One was in better condition than most though, and Keph grabbed him by the arm.

'Run to Jerl and tell him to make the gap,' he ordered.

'Gap, sir?'

'Do it! Tell Jerl to make the damn gap. Do it now, or we've already lost!'

The bemused soldier dashed away into the press of bodies. Then, slowly but surely, Jerl moved left, taking many of his soldiers with him, to squeeze Talan's flank. As the line curved and hemmed in Talan and his men, an opening appeared. Immediately Keph was on the move, hoping that he would be able to get past Gadric's men without being caught.

But he didn't have to worry: the baron was pulling his men back quickly, seeing that they were separated from their comrades, and was forming a defensive formation of his own. Keph rushed round them and started up the stairs to the first floor, the message safely in his pocket.

Then there was a collective cry of dismay from down below, and Keph looked back, hoping that either Talan or Gadric had fallen and the rebels were retreating.

Instead, he saw Jerl and Talan standing face to face, neither of them moving. Then the mass of bodies shifted, and Keph caught a glimpse of the tip of Talan's blade protruding from the back of Jerl's shoulder. The prince ripped it free and let Jerl half-stumble half-fall backwards into the waiting arms of his men. They dragged him away from the main fight to behind the battle line, but he resisted all the way. He looked up towards the stairs and saw Keph, and straight away he called for the battle line to be restored.

But as the men retreated back into position, Talan, galvanised by his victory over Jerl, surged forwards and smashed aside two soldiers before clawing his way free of the line. His men were with him in a flash, protecting their prince and shearing a huge hole in the loyalist defence.

Without hesitation, Talan sprang forwards and set upon Jerl, who had recovered enough to raise his sword, but it was slow and laboured due to his wounded shoulder.

Keph looked down and saw a small gap still between the two forces. If he was fast enough he could pick up a fallen sword, be back through the gap and help his brother.

But then the message would not reach Ostion.

He nearly went to help, but three guardsmen broke off from the main body and rushed to Jerl's aid. Confident they could overcome Talan between the four of them, Keph started up the stairs once more.

Upon reaching the top he glanced down again, and stopped dead when he saw that of the three who went to help Jerl, only one was left alive. But with a single flick of his wrist Talan sent his sword slashing across his chest, and he dropped.

In the same movement he spun inside Jerl's guard and plunged his sword into his gut, twisting it viciously before wrenching it free.

Jerl stood for a moment, swaying gently, before tumbling to the floor in a motionless heap.

Keph wanted to shout. He wanted to shout curses down on Talan until his throat was raw and all he could do was spit the blood at him. He wanted to vent his anger, but there was no anger to vent. Instead he just steadied himself against the banister as his stomach rolled and twisted like the sea crashing about in the storm. A small moan of shock escaped from his lips as he felt his knees weaken and buckle underneath him. A trickle of cold sweat ran down his forehead and into his eye, sending a sharp sting through his entire body. It was only through sheer willpower that he prevented himself from vomiting. His heart pounded in his ears, and small silver spots began to dance on the edges of his vision, and he collapsed to floor as he waited for the feeling to pass.

He didn't know how long he waited. He couldn't tell. Everything seemed to happen so slowly as the sounds of the battle below faded and merged into a continual, muffled humming on the edges of hearing. It was only when his eyes dried and his stomach stopped ripping itself apart from the inside that he moved again. He stood up on weak legs and started to make his way towards the window above the front door, where Commander Ostion would be waiting.

The commander received him with something of a surprised expression, which turned to concern upon seeing Keph's physical state. He ordered Keph to sit down, which he only did after handing Ostion the message. Ostion opened it, caught the key as it dropped out, and read Fadrinar's last order. As he read, his lips curled into a smile and his eyes lit up.

'Good Gods!' he exclaimed upon finishing it. 'The man's a genius!' He turned to a messenger. 'Run down and tell Jerl to pull back to the entrance to Fadrinar's tower.'

'Jerl is dead, commander,' Keph interrupted. 'Talan killed him.' The sick feeling and the tears returned. 'He fought my brother and three others all at once. And he killed them all. He killed my brother, commander. He took from me the only thing I had left in this world. I still don't want to believe he's dead.'

'I know, lad,' Ostion said roughly, pulling Keph to his feet. 'I know. He's not the first good soldier I've lost, and he won't be the last either. Fadrinar tells me you're his best Segrata agent, but right now you don't look like it. So pull it together now and we can grieve later. That's a promise.'

There was no arguing with the honesty in his voice, or the sincerity in his eyes. Keph nodded and steadied his breathing.

'So what now, commander?'

'We follow Fadrinar's last order. That man's a genius. Now come on. Let's go and win ourselves a battle!'

Chapter 14.

Commander Ostion gathered his two hundred men and left his vantage point. Keph stumbled along with them as they followed Ostion at a run, down the stairs into the main hall.

By now what few defenders that were left had been backed into a corner and were being hemmed in by Gadric. Talan had regrouped his men and started off into the rest of the wing, leaving a large opening in the hall into which Ostion charged.

He and his men crashed into the back of Gadric's company, decimating at least a score before the baron was able to coordinate his men enough to retreat and prevent themselves being encircled. But when Gadric broke off, Keph could see that he was limping from a slash to his leg. As he pulled away with what was left of his company, he sent a stabbing glare towards Keph, who could only respond with a blank stare of his own.

The men just rescued joined Ostion's forces, taking the number up to a little over two hundred and fifty. As one tight cohort they followed their commander, none of them save him knowing where they were going or why they were going there. All they knew was that if Ostion told them to follow him, they followed him.

The commander stopped when they came to the entrance to the Segrata tower.

'Open it, Keph,' he ordered. 'Then stand aside.'

Keph pulled out his key and stepped close to the door. As he fitted it to the lock, the side door to the wing at the end of the corridor was thrown back off its hinges as Locan and Borden burst through, leading the remaining five hundred rebels.

'Hold position!' Ostion shouted. 'Be ready to withdraw on my command!'

Upon seeing the defenders, Borden raised his crossbow and sent a bolt flying towards Ostion, but his aim was bad and his shot hasty, and it skimmed past the commander's head, skittering at a sharp angle off the wall behind him to come to a halt at Keph's feet.

'Shields up!' the Ostion cried. 'Don't die until I tell you to.'

As Borden fitted a second bolt to his crossbow, Locan led the rebels forward at a sprint, seeking to flatten the first line and cause havoc in amongst the rest.

But he was repelled as Ostion and his men held firm, striking back only if there was a safe opportunity. They did not have to hold for long though; Keph's fingers fumbled with the key a few times from the pressure of the situation and the continuing nausea caused by Jerl's death, but he fitted it on the seventh time and clicked the door open.

'Commander,' he said. 'It's open.'

'Good man,' Ostion replied without looking round. 'Pull back slowly!' he shouted. 'Don't let your guard down, and stay alert. Move!'

He turned and moved onto the landing inside the tower, taking the key from Fadrinar's order and putting it in the lock of the door leading upwards. It turned smoothly and easily, and the door swung open.

'Up the stairs,' the commander ordered. 'And don't stop moving until you're at the top.'

It was a slow retreat. The tightness of the spiral made the ascent steep and dizzying. It was not made any easier for those men who were still having to fight the rebels at the back of the retreat. They coordinated with each other so that they moved backwards up the stairs in unison to prevent the line from breaking and the rebels having an opening. After a while, only the last few ranks stayed in formation, while the others broke and turned, heading forwards up the stairs instead to catch up with Ostion and Keph.

There was no door at the top of the stairs, but an archway instead, which opened out into a long, narrow room with one side made entirely from glass. It looked out over the city and onwards to the horizon.

Next to the window was what appeared to be a telescope of some sort, mounted on a swivel axis and tilted up towards the sky. Along the other wall was a series of work benches and large tables, each one laden with designs and drawings or boxes full of tools and strange-looking compounds. There was a second archway at the far end of the room, which led to another set of spiral stairs that descended into an unknown sector of the wing. The floor of the room was scorched in dozens of places, as was the wall.

'What is this place?' said a soldier close to Keph.

'Search me,' Ostion replied. 'But this is where Fadrinar has told us to be, so here's where we'll be. Now get to guarding the entrance. I don't want anyone getting in while we do what Fadrinar has instructed. Keph, come with me. The rest of you, hold here. And stay here until I say otherwise.'

'What are we looking for, commander?' asked Keph.

'Fadrinar says he's rigged this entire wing to collapse. He's been obtaining small portions of the king's supply of black powder for years. It seemed he had his own series of secret passages he didn't even tell his Segrata about, with explosives inside every single one of them. All the fuses lead back to this room – if we can set them off and then get out, the whole wing is going to come down on top of the rebels.'

'The entire wing!' Keph stopped short. 'How is that possible?'

'Fadrinar was more intelligent than he looked, and more so than he made out he was. He was a marvel, Keph. An absolute strategic and logistical marvel. If he says he can make the whole wing go down, everything's already in place and even in death he will be true to his word. He says something about the fuse being the lion's tail, whatever that means. Sometimes I wish he would speak plainly. Now find that fuse!'

Keph set off towards the far end at a run, planning to work back into the middle of the room, where Ostion was working from one wall to the next in a lateral path.

The clang and ring of steel on steel could be heard clearly now as the rebel attack reached the defensive line at the top of the stairs. Without slowing, Locan threw himself into the fray, and in a moment had killed two defenders in as many strokes of his huge blade. Even with the deaths of two men a small gap opened up, and Locan pushed into it, and within only seconds of the initial engagement the defenders had been split open and were in disarray.

They scattered under the pressure and broke away in all directions, allowing the rebels to flood into the room.

'Damn you all, you cowards!' Ostion roared, drawing his sword and stepping in to fight the rebels. 'Find that fuse, Keph, if it's the last thing you do!'

Then he disappeared among the swirling mass of bodies.

Keph began to run as he searched, pulling benches away from the wall and rummaging through every box of tools, trying desperately to work out what Fadrinar had meant by the lion's tail. Every now and again he would look up briefly to make sure nobody was charging towards him as his frantic search took him closer and closer to the desperate melee.

By now Ostion had rallied his men into something of a defence, but against the numbers of the rebels it was not going to last long. Locan led the assault as he had done relentlessly since breaking in through the side door, and Borden stayed off to the side, picking off men from the flanks of the defensive line with deadeye shots from his crossbow. Keph could see that the elder of the princes was working his way around the side of the line, and soon he would have the space needed to shoot at Keph.

His search quickened as he worked his way right to the back of the defence, but without success. He glanced over his shoulder again and saw Borden step round the end of the line and raise his crossbow to his shoulder, aiming straight for him.

Without caring where he ended up, Keph ran, trying to find both a place to hide from Borden and the start of the black powder's fuse. He threw himself behind a large box of tools as the crossbow bolt thudded into its side.

He was about to run again and look for somewhere better situated, when he saw, only feet away from him, a small sculpture of a lion. On first glance it appeared to be made out of lengths of horsehair, bound together and then intertwined to form the shape of the lion. But Keph squinted closer, and saw that the entire sculpture was in fact made from fuses. One of the paws looked as though it was reaching through the wall itself, and the tail was curled around its feet.

Disregarding his own safety now, Keph stood up and called to Ostion.

'Commander!' he cried. 'It's here!'

'Then set the damn thing off before we all die!' the commander shouted in reply, before disappearing once again in the chaos.

But Borden had seen it too, and, throwing his crossbow to one side, he leaped at Keph, dragging him to the floor with a loud thud.

'Don't even think about lighting that,' he growled. 'You don't know what it's connected to.'

'It's connected to a whole series of explosive charges,' Keph said. 'If I light that this entire wing comes down on top of us.'

Immediately Borden reached for his belt and pulled out his knife. He thrust it towards Keph, but in Keph's struggle to break free the blade missed. He heaved Borden off him and pushed himself upright, searching for a way to light the fuse now that he had found it. But before he could find a solution Borden had once again bundled him to the floor and was pinning his arms.

'My father was right about you,' the prince snarled. 'You were a spy, and you had almost convinced me that you weren't. I'd be willing to bet my right arm you're Segrata too.'

'You'd be right. And even without Fadrinar we're not as helpless as we seem.'

His head whipped up and slammed into Borden's chin. The prince recoiled and reeled backwards, but did not let go of Keph, who bucked and writhed in an attempt to get something free. Once again Borden reached for his discarded knife, but Keph was quicker, grabbing Borden's arm as it moved towards the hilt and using it to pull him off balance. Keph took the opportunity and pushed again, sending the prince into the glass window beside them.

With a terrifying chink it cracked into a spider's web of little jagged lines, and Borden scrambled away quickly before he could be pushed into it again.

'Borden!'

Locan's suddenly panicked voice was clearly audible over the fighting. Both Keph and Borden looked round to see Locan surrounded by

Ostion and two others, and it was clear that even the big prince's skill and strength combined could not keep them at bay for much longer.

Borden stood, stunned, as he watched his brother start to falter and Ostion press the advantage. Keph could see his mind running over the possibilities. Then Borden turned towards him, and Keph saw in his eyes that he was resigned.

'Light it then, damn you,' he cursed, then drew his sword and ran to help Locan.

Keph needed no further encouragement. He glanced round desperately for something to light the fuse with. As he spun in his haste, he knocked a box of tools from a table beside him. They clattered around his feet as they fell, revealing, among their contents, two small pieces of flint.

He knew how to create a spark with flint, but had never tried it.

Well, he said to himself. *There's always a first time for everything.*

The positioning was awkward, having to get the spark to land exactly on the tip of the lion's tail, but after a few hurried strikes, the spark flew and lit the fuse. The flame fizzed to life, racing along the intertwined fuses in a sparkling frenzy. In seconds the flames had consumed the lion and disappeared along its arm and into the wall, leaving only a few small piles of ash in its wake.

Keph turned to tell Ostion of his success, but upon turning he saw Borden reach Locan and the commander, and stab his sword into Ostion's back. The commander crumpled, landing on the wooden floor with an ominous thud.

Already the first of the shudders was echoing through the wing, and small chunks of stone were dropping from the walls and ceiling.

'Pull back!' Keph cried. 'Back to the north wing! We can do no more here!'

He led the retreat as it scattered from the fight and ran towards the archway at the far end of the room. The tight spiral stairs made for a treacherous descent, especially as the men at the back were pushing those in front to go faster, causing a few of them to stumble and almost trip on their way down. Keph leaped down them three at a time, constantly steadying himself on the central pillar as the entire wing shook and groaned as Fadrinar's explosives shattered its weak points.

They reached the bottom in a tumble of bodies, and dashed along the corridor to the door at the far end. Keph wrenched it open and ran into the space beyond.

They were in the courtyard, but on the opposite side of the wing to the side door. As the last of the men escaped the wing they looked back to see where their door was, only to find that it had swung shut again, leaving a solid wall of stone behind them.

'Come on!' Keph urged them. 'If we stay too close we'll be caught in it as well. Let's go!'

Once again they began to run, this time with a little more freedom and space, charging across the courtyard until they were safely in the shadow of the north wing, the only part of the palace that remained completely in the king's control. Once there, they turned once more and watched as the entire west wing collapsed in on itself in a cloud of ash and dust and an avalanche of stone, wood and broken glass.

While the men around him watched the building collapse, Keph turned his attention towards the east wing, where the remainder of the rebels watched with similar horror and disbelief. Gadric was there, leaning on Borden for support as he gazed incredulously at Fadrinar's handiwork. Locan sported only a few scratches, though he was only alive through his brother's efforts. Prince Talan was nowhere to be seen. Of the two thousand soldiers Gadric had brought with him from Bronze Keep, only three hundred remained alive. But it was still more than the number of Ostion's men who had survived.

Barely fifty men under Ostion's command had left the west wing alive. The commander was dead, his body smashed and broken, somewhere among the wreckage.

And so was Jerl's.

Chapter 15.

King Cassien's throne room had always been his favourite place to sit in times of trouble. The throne stood on a three-tier dais at the far end of the room, its back tall and tapering to a sharp point. The silver frame and arms were as polished as mirrors, so much so that they seemed almost transparent, as if a person could look at them and see what lay beyond. The seat and back were cushioned with a soft red lining, though it was starting to fray at the edges from its constant use. The dais was framed by a large pillar on each corner, engraved with intertwining vines that spread out onto the roof and onto the floor. Around the top of the walls ran a gantry that encompassed the whole room, with doors leading onto it from the floor above.

Cassien sat slumped in the throne, his forehead resting on his clenched fist. Keph stood in front of him, waiting for the king to vent his anger.

'Tell me, Keph,' the king said, slowly. 'Why did you disobey my order and leave the rebels' camp? Was it because you wanted to spite me? Or were you arrogant enough to want me to see your initiative and independence?'

'Neither, my liege,' Keph replied. Though he was resolved to tell Cassien the exact truth of his actions, he did not even dare to hope that the king would accept them.

'Then why did you disobey me? Why did you defy your king?'

'Because the rebels had me under guard, my liege,' Keph explained. 'They believed I was a spy for you, and rather than risk me walking free they put me under guard until the rebellion was over.'

'And what did you do that made them suspect you were my spy?'

'As far as I am aware, my liege, I had done nothing to give them such a notion. It seemed that Baron Gadric would have distrusted me anyway, being one of your servants in his family's service.'

'You dare to tell me that it was I who did my job wrongly?' Cassien's voice became even slower, quieter, and more dangerous. Keph knew that even choosing his words carefully would be no defence against the king's impending fury.

'No, my liege. I merely explain how Gadric's natural distrust of anything associated with you and your household has led to his increasing paranoia.'

'And so not content with disobeying your king, you now present yourself to me as a man who presumes to know how the mind works of someone so highly above his station. The impertinence.'

Cassien looked up and placed his chin on his fist now instead of his forehead.

'I used to believe, once upon a time, that you were trustworthy,' he said quietly. 'I used to believe that I had people around me who felt I was worth serving, that I was worth being loyal to, that my service gave them something in this world that nothing else could. I used to believe that I was a king who was respected by his people and loved by those same people. And yet in my own court, in my own palace, in my own family there are people who hate me, who disrespect me so much that they think they can defy me without consequence. There will be consequences, Keph. Of that I can assure you. And you and Jessa will feel the full force of them.'

'What about the rebels, my liege? Gadric and his family? What about them?'

'There was never any trust between us, not even before that battle that drew us apart. When he showed his true colours I never felt as though I had lost anything or been betrayed. Not like with you and Jessa. I once respected both of you for the people you were, and I gave you my favour. But now, she has thrown it all back at me by siding with my enemy. And you, Keph . . . I respected you as well. Fadrinar always said you were a strong, reliable agent. And now, when I give you the ultimate task of doing all you can to protect your king, you too throw it all back at me by taking it upon yourself to do what *you* think is right.'

'At the time, my liege, it seemed the only logical course of action,' Keph said. Then he braced himself for the inevitable onslaught.

'And exactly how is defying your king, who had given you the order *personally*, the most logical course of action? You might pretend to understand those of us who are so clearly beyond you in intellect and authority, but I do not have the arrogance to pretend to understand you. You are the one who has to explain yourself to me, not me to you. *Never* will I have to explain myself to the likes of you! Now tell me *why* you defied me!'

Keph let Cassien's rage stop echoing off the walls before he attempted to explain.

'I was practically their prisoner, my liege. There was nothing that I could do to get close enough to the leaders to make any sort of difference. I heard, through listening to the soldiers around me, that the next target would be the Segrata, and there had been an assurance to the men that the Segrata would be out of the way before they began the attack on the west wing the following morning. I concluded that it would be an evening assassination attempt of some kind on Commissar Fadrinar, and it seemed to me that I had only two choices: to remain a prisoner and let the Segrata be destroyed, or escape and warn the commissar myself.'

The king looked at him doubtfully.

'I'm sure it seemed like the best thing for you to do, and under normal circumstances I might have been lenient enough to forgive you. However, not only have you disobeyed me, you have destroyed one full quarter of my palace. Without my permission. I would call that an attack against the king.'

By now Keph was having difficulty controlling himself.

'If you did that, my liege, we would have to disagree.'

'Oh? And so you defy me again. It seems your insolence knows no bounds. I think, however, that I am right in saying that you are not the man I thought you were. You first came to my attention before the Segrata was set up. I already knew you had . . . defining . . . qualities about you that were not present in my other servants. I knew that there was something different about you that brought you to my attention. At the time I thought it was dedication to your work and to me, your willingness to serve, and your ability to get on well with anyone.'

The king laughed.

'But I see now, after all these years, that I was wrong. I have been the butt end of your deception, and now you will answer for it. I see now that those defining qualities were not dedication and willingness. No. They were subterfuge and deceit and arrogance. You played me well, getting me to give you a post in my secret police, and all along you knew that you would gain my full and complete trust, and then throw it all aside and defy me when I am at my weakest. Oh, yes. You played me very well.'

'My liege, I must protest now,' Keph snapped. 'I have served you faithfully from the first day I entered your service, and I have only ever done what I have believed and felt to be right. The destruction of the west wing was not my idea. If someone must be blamed for it, then the blame lies with Commissar Fadrinar. He was the one who prepared everything. Commander Ostion and I only found out after his death what he had done.'

'Fadrinar did this?' The king stiffened in his throne. 'And here I thought he was one of the few people left who was loyal to me.'

'He was loyal,' Keph said. 'He was fanatically loyal. He made a sacrifice of part of your palace so that you could be kept safe.'

'Sacrifice?' Cassien spat. 'I fail to see how obliterating my guard's headquarters qualifies as a method of keeping me safe.'

'The explosion was devastating enough to take a few hundred of the rebels with it. As far as I am aware, Prince Talan and his men did not escape. At least, I did not see them after it collapsed.'

'And you expect me to believe that it did any good? We are still vastly outnumbered!'

'But not by anywhere near as big a margin as we would have been had the wing not been destroyed.'

'Had Commander Ostion retreated when it was safest and most tactically sound to do so,' Cassien said firmly, 'we would have a two hundred more men and their commander with which to repel the rebels. Now what do we have? Fifty battle-weary soldiers and my own few bodyguards. That isn't even sixty men.'

'True, my liege,' said Keph, 'but if we had not destroyed the wing, they would have had three hundred men more than they have now. They have half the number of men left that they could have had.'

'But my point remains,' Cassien insisted. 'All this was done without consulting me. You, and Ostion, and Fadrinar, and Jessa have all gone behind my back and betrayed me in some way. Do you have any idea what it's like to have so many people who you trusted suddenly turn around and betray you? Do you have any idea what it's like to be the king who tries to help his people and has things thrown back at his face in return? You have no idea what it's like, so do not even try to judge me or understand me or console me, because you do not have the authority.'

He calmed down slightly, breathing heavily.

'This is the biggest loss I have suffered since the death of my brother. I could expect you to understand, but it would be a foolish thing to hope for.' The king shook his head wearily. 'You don't know what it's like to lose a brother, Keph, and I won't try explaining it to someone as low and as petty as you.'

'My liege, my brother died defending the west wing. I do know what it's like to lose a brother. I do, so don't pretend that we can't feel alike, because we are, my liege. We are alike. We have both had to suffer the loss of a brother. Being king doesn't make that feeling of loss and of grief any different to what I feel.'

'If I had any sympathy left I might be upset at your loss,' Cassien said quietly. 'But I have none for you. I see now that anything I give to anyone except myself is undeserved. You tell me your brother is dead, and you feel it as keenly as I do, but you lie. You can't tell what it's like to lose a brother who *actually* loves you, a brother who you *actually* love. Did your brother love you? No. Did you love him? Of course not. You were both too simple for that.'

'My liege – '

'If you loved your brother as much as I loved mine, you would be grieving for him!' Cassien roared, leaping out of his throne and bearing down on Keph, who only narrowly resisted the urge to back away in fear. 'If you loved your brother as much as I loved mine, you would be on the floor weeping for him! If you had loved your brother, you would have gone to the grave with him!'

He brought his face close Keph's and lowered his voice to a venomous whisper.

'Now leave me in peace. Leave this room. Leave this city. Leave my service and never return, otherwise I swear I will put you in the ground myself.'

Chapter 16.

Keph left the king's throne room, sullen and tired. The king's last words still rang in his ears.

Leave my service and never return, otherwise I swear I will put you in the ground myself.

Until that conversation, such as it was, Keph had always looked up to the king, had always respected him and never doubted him, and now Cassien was betraying that faith that Keph had placed in him. If anyone was being betrayed, it was Keph. Not the king. As far as Keph was concerned, the king had caused others to betray him. It had been his fault that they hated him so much, but he could not . . . would not . . . see that.

And to be told that he did not love Jerl, and that Jerl did not love him, was devastating. All good opinion he had had of Cassien was gone. The king had caused Keph to lose all respect for him. His arrogance and conceit had blinded him to the truth and caused him to send away one of the few people who had still been willing to serve him no matter how grave the situation became.

Keph wanted to feel something different, something other than hate and disgust, but it was impossible. He could not stop the bitter thoughts that circled round and round in his head. He could not stop the rage and the fury that pulsated through him as he walked, not knowing or caring where to. He felt the anger rise inside him and flood straight into his heart.

He forgot how to forgive, how to love, how to feel. All he knew was how to reject and how to curse . . . and how to hate. Now more than ever he wanted to take up a sword and stab it through Cassien's heart and into his soul, and leave it there for him to feel as he died.

'You look angry, Keph,' said a voice in the nearby doorway.

Keph spun round and saw that Deel was watching him from the open door of his room. In his blind bitterness he had ended up at Deel's quarters.

'If you were me,' he said darkly, 'you would look angry too.'

'Then let me be a friend; come and talk to me about it,' Deel said cheerfully, though his cheeriness was not returned.

'I won't put you through that,' Keph said. 'Just let me be.'

'Can't do that, old friend,' Deel replied quickly. 'Bad conscience on my part. Come on, come in. Tell me your troubles, and perhaps I can find a way to alleviate them.'

Keph knew it would be rude of him to walk away now, especially when Deel was being so friendly and open. He followed the playwright into his room and shut the door behind him.

'I hear the king's been having problems with rebels,' Deel remarked. 'Baron Gadric, I think. Bad business. Bad for writing, and bad for finding actors to act.'

'If this play of yours ever gets performed,' said Keph, 'then count yourself lucky. In a few days, everything here will be over, one way or another Not that I really care anymore.'

'Don't talk like a pessimist until you actually are one,' said Deel. 'And you can't be a pessimist until I am. That's what friends are for: getting down and upset before everyone else so that everyone else feels better about themselves.'

'If I cared enough to try to understand you, I'd ask you to run that by me again,' Keph said. 'But the truth is I'm past caring.'

'Now before you go all depressed and take your own life – '

'I'm not going to go that far.'

'Then before you go and get all depressed,' Deel continued, 'why don't you hear me out? Let me talk to you and tell you something. Let me tell you a story, Keph.'

'Deel – '

'Humour me. Go on.'

Deel took his silence as a consent.

'Now,' he said gently. 'A few years ago, I was out in the town, looking for some actors to put on my play. Do you remember that comedy I wrote a few years back about a pair of twins who get shipwrecked and the girl dresses as a boy and falls in love and there are all sorts of mix ups? Well, it was that one. Anyway, I was looking for some actors to do it, and in one of the slightly less reputable inns I found a man who looked almost as down as you are. So I spoke to him, and I told him something, and almost immediately he cheered up.'

'Why was he so down?' Keph asked.

'Because he'd reached the bottom of his drink.'

'Then whatever it is you're about to try on me won't work. I have much bigger problems than that.'

'Like what? Nothing you can say will surprise me. Just say it plainly and let me see what I can make of it.'

'Jerl is dead and the king has released me from service. He has told me to leave the city and never return.'

Deel took this in silently, and Keph immediately regretted what he had said, wondering if he had done the right thing by telling Deel. He knew that Deel would understand, but whether he could help was another problem entirely. In Keph's experience, some things were better left to be sorted out by the person they concerned instead of that person's friend.

'Clearly there's more to this than meets the eye,' Deel said at length. 'Tell me all, Keph. Tell me everything.'

It was with some trepidation and unease that Keph recounted the start of the rebellion, his appointment to Borden and the king's order regarding it, the escape to warn Fadrinar, Fadrinar's death, the attack on the west wing, Jerl's death, Ostion's death and the king's reaction. As he spoke he saw Deel listen in shock. It was the longest space of time in which he had ever known Deel to be completely silent, uttering not one single syllable until he had finished.

'Good Gods. It's all so wrong. All this killing and death and anger. I don't want to believe that the human race is so flawed, but there can be no other explanation for all this. And what the king said about you and Jerl is just plain wrong.'

'I'm glad you believe me,' Keph said. 'I was worried that if I spoke ill of the king you would not take me seriously.'

'Of all the people in this world whom I trust,' said Deel, 'I trust you most of all. The king sounds as though he has finally cracked under the pressure, and now I understand everything. I understand it all, and I wish I didn't. *Fool*, they call me. In occupation, perhaps, but in reality I consider myself among the wisest of men. The wisest of fools, even.'

He moved over to the small window on the other side of the room and looked out.

'The king is scared,' he said. 'The king has always been scared. The problem with people in positions of power, Keph, is that they always fear to lose it. The king has been a tyrant ever since the first time he sat on that throne, but we have been too blind to see it. We have been so close to him that we have been taken in by everything he has told us. There haven't been riots and bad harvests; it has been the king all along, murdering people and confiscating their food and their belongings. And since Jessa turned against him he started to lose control of what he had. His pride and joy – his niece and heir – cast him aside, and he started to believe that everyone hated him. His fear overcame him, and the first person he had to release it all onto was you.'

He turned back to face Keph.

'Have you ever considered you're on the wrong side in all this? Have you ever considered the fact that you could have been working for the wrong man all this time? All these years you have been working for Cassien, you have been working for a tyrant and a monster. Have you ever considered the possibility that Cassien is the villain of this story, and Gadric is the hero? Cassien is a tyrant. He always has been, and until he's stopped he always will be, but none of us could see that because we were too close to see. It's time to change that, Keph. If you leave, as the king has ordered you to, you will never be able to come back. You will never have made a difference, and you will never have made a stand. Don't you want to make a stand, Keph? Make a stand for what you believe in? For goodness and for justice? For Jerl?'

Keph let his words sink in, and was about to speak when Deel started again.

'Jerl died because you did what you were told to do. You delivered Ostion that message, and Jerl died because of it. If the king and Fadrinar had not been so forceful about making you follow your orders, you could have gone back down those stairs and saved your brother. It would have meant Ostion would never have got the message, and things would be different, most likely worse. But Jerl would have been alive, which is what counts.

'Borden had the same choice you did: he could either let you light that fuse and save his younger brother, or he could stop you causing havoc and allow his brother to die. He chose to save his brother, and no doubt Gadric has reprimanded him about it, but it shows how different the people are who are not so close to the tyrant that they are blind.'

'What are you trying to say, Deel?' said Keph. 'What are you driving at?'

'I see now that the king is not fit to rule this kingdom. Take a leaf out of Gadric's book. It's because of people like Cassien that Jerl died. It doesn't just happen here – I can guarantee that. It happens everywhere. There are other places in this world where people like Cassien rule irresponsibly and foolishly, costing the lives of too many of their subjects. Take a stand, Keph, and pick a side, because everybody else has . . . and if you don't, when this fight is over you will have nowhere to go and no one to turn to. There won't be anyone who will remember Jerl except you, and that is just wrong.'

'And you have already chosen a side?'

'I have. I'm packing up this instant and going to offer the baron my services, such as they are.'

'You may be able to go to the rebels and offer your services,' Keph said bitterly. 'But I'm afraid I can't. Not after what happened yesterday. Yesterday, I revealed myself as a spy for Cassien. I admitted to Borden this morning that I was with the Segrata. They won't accept me back unless I prove I've left Cassien for good, and there is no way for me to prove that. You tell me that if I don't pick a side I'll be left with nothing. I already have nothing, Deel! Nothing! No family, no job, no home now, no respect for anyone and nobody to respect me. I'm a shell, Deel. A shell of what I once was. You can't save me, so don't bother trying.'

'I'll save you even if you kill me for it,' Deel said stoutly. 'That's a promise.'

'Deel, you don't understand,' Keph insisted. 'I can't go back to Cassien, otherwise he will have me killed. I can't go back to Gadric because he knows by now I was with the Segrata. Tell me . . . where can I go? Tell me where!'

'Right now, you can't go anywhere,' Deel said patiently. 'But I promised I would save you, and save you I shall.'

He sat himself down at his desk and pulled a piece of paper towards him. He poised his quill above it, and then began to write, his lips working quicker than his hand as he muttered and murmured under his breath. Once or twice Keph attempted to get a look at what Deel was writing, but every time he moved even an inch closer the paper was slid away from him and shielded by Deel's arm or hand.

In amongst the scratch and scribble of Deel's quill, Keph resigned himself to a long, hard future with no joy or happiness or laughter to comfort him, no Jerl to accompany him on his journey, nothing to say or do, nowhere to stay or to hide. He looked into the future, trying to see past the despair and the darkness that clouded his vision, but it was so deep and so intense it became the only thing his future held. There was no end to the rolling storm clouds with their streaks of lightning and lashing rain and biting winds. A future filled with grief and despair and dark shadows at every turn was all that he could see awaiting him.

Beyond that, he wanted to believe that there would be nothing – a nameless oblivion into which he could fall whenever he wanted, but even that was too much to hope for. In the lengthening darkness, all he could see was more shadows and more barren, grey moments in his life, all of them stark and bleak.

He would leave the city, perhaps even the kingdom, and he would travel to wherever his feet took him. He didn't care where he ended up: all his futures and all his roads would be the same from now until his death, and even when he died his world would still be grey and dull. There would be no heaven for him, no paradise for his soul, no eternal peace.

Instead, he would be forever plagued by his dark and lonely life. It would be shown to him over and over and over again until it drove him to madness in his death. He would be not only dead, but his soul would have been driven to the brink of insanity and beyond by the torture of his life past.

No, there was nothing to look forward to.

'All done,' Deel said suddenly. But even so it took Keph a few seconds to drag himself back to the present. Deel rolled the piece of paper like a scroll and tied it with a crimson ribbon, before handing it to Keph.

'What is this?' Keph said.

'This is your salvation.'

Keph looked at him doubtfully, then tucked the scroll into his pocket.

'How can you be so sure?' he asked.

'Trust me,' Deel said with a roguish smile. 'Think of it as a gift, from one friend to another.'

'You don't even know I'm going to open this.'

'No, I don't. But I have faith that you will have enough sense to want to open it, once you're done moping and you're ready to face the world again. Because it's a world you deserve to live in. Count on it.'

Chapter 17.

Again, Keph wandered the halls and corridors of the north wing, not caring what or who he passed. All he wanted to do was find somewhere quiet, dark and secluded, where he could hide himself away and wish for something better, even though he knew it wouldn't help. There was nothing he cared for now except retaining his own sanity, and even then he knew that if he lost it, he wouldn't miss it. Even the conversation with Deel had done nothing to help him.

Join with Gadric and his rebels? That would never be the solution; it would only make things worse. Not for the kingdom, but for himself. Neither Cassien nor Gadric would have him: by one he was branded a traitor, and by the other a spy.

And what was left for him in Sorl?

Nothing. No friends, no job, no home.

No family, now that Jerl was dead.

The thought caught in his throat, and he half-choked half-coughed as he tried to stop himself from crying. He had never cried in front of Jerl, and he did not intend to cry over him. It would ruin the comradeship they had had, even though they were no longer together.

There wasn't even a body for him to bury.

But that might have made it even harder. With a body, one has a trigger to start the emotions and the tears once again, and make sure they never stop and never leave. And it would make him not only saddened, but hateful too. He would hate Talan and his family for what had occurred; his entire world had been changed in the space of a couple of days, and his life changed forever. If he were to hate, he knew that he would find himself saying things that were better left unsaid and doing things that were better left undone.

Besides, he didn't have the energy to hate.

A pair of guards passed him as he turned a corner, but they ignored him. He wondered if what Deel had said was true. He wondered whether even the guards had been taken in by Cassien and his deceptions, or whether they were aware of the truth but too scared or too indecisive to do anything about it. Were the rest of his servants questioning him like Deel was? Were his ministers? His wife?

If the queen was questioning him and his motives, how little support could the king have? But there was no evidence that she did question him. Perhaps, in trying to play the dutiful but resentful wife, she had let herself be taken in by Cassien's deceptions.

It was all too confusing and too difficult to tell what was what anymore. Keph had no notion what was right or what was wrong, both factually and morally. Deel had said that Keph and Borden had had the same choice, and yet they had done completely opposite things.

Why?

Should he have gone back to help Jerl? Should he have saved his brother at the expense of Fadrinar's message? Would it have made things different? Almost certainly. Would it have made things better? There was no way to tell. In doing what he had been ordered to do, Keph had ensured that the plan had worked, but he had lost his brother in the process. His younger brother, whom he had always promised to protect and be there for. And he had caused his death. It was something more than just guilt that he would have to live with.

It would be shame, too. And fire.

Fires stoked in hell itself, kindled from the sparks of fear.

It was an old story, to stop children fearing death; they were told that the fires of hell were fuelled by their fear, and by fearing death they condemned themselves to an afterlife of fire and ash in the hellish caverns beneath the earth.

But now, in the turbulent waters of despair, they seemed more real than anything else, no longer tales told by old men, but a sharp, stark reality, brighter and hotter than a branding iron.

Did Borden feel the same right now?

He had had the same option as Keph, but he had hardly stopped to make the choice. He had helped his younger brother at the expense of the attack on the west wing. He had caused the attack to fail in its aim, but he still had his brother. He probably had guilt too, but no shame and no fire to sear his soul.

Keph started in surprise as Nard appeared beside him from out of another passage.

'Steady, Keph,' the valet said. Then he looked closer. 'My goodness, you look awful.'

'So would you if you had been through what I've been through.'

'What do you mean? What's happened?'

Keph hesitated before replying; the notion had suddenly occurred to him that since Nard was with the king, perhaps he knew already what had happened, and the concern in his voice was faked, designed to lull Keph into a false sense of security before mocking him just like the king had. But the thought was gone as quickly as it had come, and he wondered at the fact he had even thought it.

'What's happened?' Nard asked again. This time, the concern and sincerity of his voice persuaded Keph that he genuinely was worried.

'Jerl is dead and the king has released me from service. He has told me to leave the city and never return.'

It was easier to say this time. It was easier to comprehend. But by no means was it easier to bear. He felt his chest constrict and his breath catch in his throat, and his jaw tightened and clenched in an effort to stay composed.

'Good Gods.' Fortunately, Nard looked away before Keph could lose complete control. 'What on earth did he release you for? Surely you of all people cannot have made him so angry?'

Not even a mention of Jerl. Was he so unconcerned by his death? Or was he not surprised? Or perhaps he just didn't want to make things any worse for Keph. Maybe he thought he was doing a good thing by not mentioning Jerl, but if Keph had felt like being honest, he would have told Nard straight away how insulted and how hurt he was that the memory of Jerl had just been brushed aside so casually.

'Of all people,' Keph replied darkly, 'I alone should make him angry. I have disobeyed his direct command and I have taken actions upon myself, so large and so devastating they have caused untold destruction, without his sanction.'

'I'm sorry –' Nard began.

'Don't be sorry for me,' Keph snapped. 'I deserve this punishment. If you're going to be sorry for anyone, Nard, be sorry for Jerl. He's the one that's dead! He made a sacrifice for something he believed in, something he truly and utterly believed in. What sacrifice have you made for your king and your kingdom? What have you sacrificed for the people and the land you love? Absolutely nothing! So don't be sorry for me, or for yourself, or even for the king! Because out of everybody in this palace, my brother, who I loved as dearly as a brother can, has been killed.'

He saw that his words were having an effect on Nard; the valet's mouth was still open, and his eyes were suddenly soft and downcast. But Keph had begun now to release all his pent up anger, and had no intention of stopping until it was all gone, regardless of whom he directed it at or how he hurt or insulted them.

'My brother,' he shouted, 'is dead! The last thing I had left in this world has been torn away from me, and nothing is ever going to bring him back. Never again will I see him, speak to him, laugh with him. He gave his life for his king, and for his kingdom, and the very king he died to protect has condemned his actions and convicted his brother. What sort of king does that make him? It doesn't make him king, it can't. No true king can have it within his heart to be so ruthlessly arrogant that he fails to recognise faithful and dutiful service and sacrifice.'

'You're starting to sound like the rebels,' Nard said quietly, clearly trying to calm Keph down, but avoid his rage at the same time. Neither worked.

'So what if I do? As far as I can see, the rebels seem to have the right idea. I've seen now how much of a tyrant Cassien is, and how little he cares for his subjects. To be honest, Nard, I don't give a damn what happens here now. The king has exiled me, and the rebels know me to have been his spy. I have nowhere to go, Nard. Nothing to do, no one to be with. You and me . . . we're both servants and we're both Segrata. We both know what it's like to serve, and to be loyal. Loyalty is something more and more people are lacking these days. We both know what it's like to look up to someone the way we looked up to the king. But what you *don't* know, what you have absolutely *no idea* about, is how it feels to have that king betray you.'

'Keph –'

'Shut up. You told me, when we were out on that hunting trip with the king and Prince Borden, that you had served the king since he was eighteen, and that though he did strange and questionable things, he always had a valid reason for them. Do you think he has a valid reason for this? In an extremely short space of time he insulted me, my loyalty, my integrity, and my brother. In fact, he insulted Jerl in even more ways than he insulted me. That is something that can *never* have a valid reason, Nard, and nothing you can say or do will ever convince me otherwise.

'Do you know what Deel is doing?' Keph continued, watching with savage relish how his words were biting deep into Nard as the valet tried to keep his own composure. 'Deel – the poet, the playwright, the fool – is packing up his belongings and going to join the rebels because he has decided the king has gone too far. He has seen me at my worst, and he has seen what the king has done to me, and he is going to do something about it. He is going to join with the people who really, truly, care for the people they rule over. If you had any sense you would do the same. It seems futile to stay with the king.'

'But the king –'

'If you're going to tell me the king is a good man or a great leader who will see this through to victory,' Keph said sharply, 'don't bother. The king is a broken man, Nard. He is a broken man who has lost not only his faith but his sanity. He has had his niece betray him, and he believes that I, Commander Ostion and Commissar Fadrinar betrayed him too. He is a broken man, Nard. He's not the king, not the man, he once was. Let your loyalty for him go, and see for yourself what he truly is. He's a shell of his former self.'

Keph stopped, suddenly overcome with tiredness, and he realised just how weary and how spent he was. He stopped his ranting and closed his eyes, trying to clear his mind of all the thoughts of anger and rage enough to think properly. In this silence, Nard said,

'But what about you? What are you going to do? Where will you go? I hate to see a man of your calibre go walking into the shadows and just disappear from the world.'

'A man of my calibre,' muttered Keph. 'My calibre is spent now. I tried to do what I believed was the right thing to do, and I failed to make it work. I think it's time I walked into the shadows. I'll find somewhere dark and secluded and out of the way where I can spend the rest of my sorry life without having to worry about anything or anyone else. I will finally be free.'

'That's an evil thought, Keph,' said Nard. 'That's an evil thought in evil times, when we're surrounded by evil people. I have never wanted to see a man think, let alone say, such things. I suppose I can't stop you leaving, but I can at least try to help you before you go.'

'And exactly how do you expect to be able to help me now? Deel tried to help, and all he ended up doing was writing something for me to read whenever I like. Some help.'

'You and Deel are good friends, and I expect he was trying to make you see reason and go with him to join Gadric and his rebels. But I'm a little more realistic than Deel, so I'm going to tell you to make sure than when you leave here, you make sure you're happy and you're safe. You're a good man at heart, Keph, but you're going through evil times. Don't let those thoughts of yours take over, otherwise I can guarantee you will end up just the same as the king: a shell of a man, broken and empty. For Jerl if for no one else, just be happy, and be safe. Can you do that, Keph? For Jerl?'

At first Keph's response would have been to deny the help and continue with his gloominess until it became all he knew in life. But at the mention of Jerl he stopped himself and listened properly for the first time since his argument with Cassien, less than an hour before. He could see the strings Nard was pulling, and he didn't want to go with it, but knew that not to accept Nard's suggestion would be to insult Jerl, and that was something Keph had always been resolved never to do.

'Alright,' he said, looking away, anxious to avoid Nard's gaze. 'Alright. I'll do it. I'll get my belongings and spend the night in the city, maybe in one of the inns. Then I'll be on my way in the morning. For Jerl. But do me a favour in return, Nard.'

'Anything.'

'Think about this whole affair very seriously. I was being serious when I told you it would be better to join the rebels. I really was. I don't expect you to do it just because I told you to, but in times like these a man needs to start thinking of himself sometimes. Do me a favour and really think hard. I want what's best for people, even if I can't have it for myself.'

'I'll do that,' Nard said. 'I'll think about that. And good luck to you, Keph. I wish you all the best. I really do. Both for your sake, and for Jerl's.'

Chapter 18.

Keph returned to his room, tired, cold and numb. He glanced over to the bed in which he had slept for nine years. It had seen better days, but it was still serviceable nonetheless. In his melancholy he briefly entertained the idea of taking it with him, or at least taking the sheets; though thin and fraying, they still felt warm and homely to him. But as he looked around what had been his home for the past nine years, he was suddenly aware of exactly how little he owned. All he had to his name was a few sets of servant's clothes, a couple of sets of casual clothes for use in the city, the woollen cloak he had pinched from his father when he was a kid, a small backpack and a tiny flick-knife given to him upon his entry into the Segrata.

For nine years he had lived in the king's palace, serving and waiting on him, cooking for him, and he had been for so long in such high society that he had forgotten exactly how poor and how low he was. He had been a servant. At the end of the day, that was all it came down to: he had spent his adult life as a servant from a poor family, but in the richest place in the kingdom, and he had believed himself to be well-off.

The irony was almost poetic.

It would be hard to leave the room for the last time, taking with him only what he could make use of in his backpack, but he had had to say goodbye to everything else: his job, Deel, Nard . . . Jerl. It was just one more thing that he would leave behind as a memory of happier times, and once he left that behind, he would have nothing left of his old life save a few memories. In time, he might forget what the kitchen looked like, or the way the head chef talked, or shouted, but he knew that deep down he would never forget the king, and how he had wilfully deceived everyone who knew and trusted him, and how he had so insulted Keph in their last meeting.

But even more than that, he knew that he would never . . . ever . . . forget Jerl.

With a resigned heart and tired eyes, Keph changed into one of his sets of street clothes and packed the other into the backpack, along with the woollen cloak. He put the flick-knife in his pocket so that it was easily in reach, and looked around to see if he had missed anything.

But then, that was being hopeful.

And then another thought struck him.

I don't have a single coin to my name.

It had always been his policy to live life to the full; whenever he had got his monthly pay he had gone out into the city and spent it. He had gambled and drunk and eaten like a king for a few days before going back to having nothing. After all, he didn't have to pay lodgings or taxes being in the king's employ, and he had never seen the need to save, having been promised continued employment in the king's services as long as his affiliation with the Segrata continued. And to leave the Segrata had always been an option synonymous with signing one's own death warrant.

And so once again he stopped, this time in the doorway to what had been his room, and he wondered where he would go and what he would do. He had no connections of any use, no money, and not even anything worth exchanging in return for what he needed. The king had told him to leave the city, but where could he go? It seemed impossible that there was anywhere he could go unless he had money or something else on him that he could use to barter with.

Even though time and again he had promised himself he wouldn't, he stood and cried, closing his eyes and letting the tears slide down his cheeks. He didn't choke or sniff or whimper, but stood still and motionless and let his tears run until there were none left. One or two trickled into his mouth and splashed onto his tongue, and their bitter taste left him angry at his lack of composure. But he could do nothing to stop the tears now that they had started.

He didn't know how long he stood there, with his backpack slung on his back and his tears dripping onto the floor where he stood. All he knew was that now he had started to be rid of all the sorrow and grief that had been building up inside him the past few hours, he didn't want to stop. He wanted to be free of it, to let it all out, let it go. He wanted to leave and start his new life without anything to hinder him, and yet even though he stood there long after he had stopped crying, he still couldn't get rid of that feeling of guilt that gnawed away inside him, right at the centre of his soul, until it became almost so tangible it felt real, as though something within him was eating away at his insides.

Eventually, he opened his eyes and looked around one last time at the room in which he had lived for so much of his life.

Then he turned abruptly and left, knowing that if he stayed a moment longer he would do worse than cry.

Once he got moving, he felt better, though by no means completely recovered. But at least he had something to do now, with a purpose in mind. He was going to leave the palace and make for his most frequent inn, on the southern side of the city. He and the landlord had always got along fairly well with each other, and Keph was hoping that he could get a night free as a favour between friends, and then start off from the city the next morning. Exactly where he was going to head for after that, he had no idea.

He left the north wing and crossed the courtyard to the palace gate, expecting it to be under the king's control still, but instead it was guarded by a pair of Gadric's soldiers, who barred his way as he made for the gate.

'Where are you going?' they demanded.

'I'm leaving,' Keph replied coldly. 'I'm leaving here and never returning.'

Clearly he had said something the guards had not anticipated. After a brief pause, in which Keph stood staring into their blank faces, they said,

'Empty your backpack. And your pockets, too.'

Knowing it was better to comply than to resist, he did as he was bidden. He emptied out his backpack, but in doing so made sure he concealed the small flick-knife up his sleeve, just in case, leaving nothing in his pockets. The guards looked over what few possessions he had, and then chuckled.

'Can't blame you for leaving, if that's all you have here,' they said. 'Go on, get going. We don't want to kill innocents.'

As Keph passed them on his way out of the gate, he said quietly, unsure whether they could hear him or not,

'I'm not innocent.'

It was true; he felt the guilt of having let Jerl die, because he could have saved him if he had only acted quicker. But that was all in the past, and as much as he wished he didn't have to think about it anymore, in amongst his brief thoughts of guilt, something that Nard had said came back to him.

That's an evil thought, Keph. That's an evil thought in evil times, when we're surrounded by evil people.

Evil? Was there anything in this world so strong that it could be evil? Such a violent, bold word. And yet when he thought about the fact that he was guilty, he had to ask himself what he was guilty of. Letting his brother die. That was the obvious answer. But what exactly was that? Was it evil to have let Jerl be killed? Is that why he had felt so wretched and so sick – because he had been evil, done an evil thing?

And by extent, what did that make Borden? Was he 'good' because he had saved his brother and not let his orders get in the way? Was he now the very embodiment of what it meant to have a good and pure soul with no taint or dishonour?

No, he told himself quickly. *The world isn't split into black and white like that. The world doesn't deal with absolutes. I'm not evil. I can't be.*

No, he wasn't evil. He had decided he was not . . . could not . . . be evil. Not in a world where people did things for so many different reasons and never really knew what they were doing or where they were going, where they would end up. It was a grey world which blurred the lines between what was right and what was wrong. That was why Cassien had been able to get away with his atrocities for so long.

Only now, when things had become so bad, did Keph finally begin to understand.

The city was silent as he walked. The last of the shop owners had closed up and gone back to their rooms above their shops. The workers in the mason's yard and the carpentry quarter had finished their work and returned home for the night. Back to their families and their friends. The market traders had closed down their stalls and retired for the evening, ready to set up once again the next morning and stand and shout all day long for people to come and buy their goods. The last of the children had been gathered back inside by their mothers, and the doors locked and curtains drawn across the windows.

He wondered exactly how much these people – these normal, innocent people – knew about what was happening in the palace. Surely they knew that Baron Gadric and his retinue had arrived a few days earlier, but whether word had got out of the rebellion against the king was another matter. Those few people Keph saw in the streets and alleys seemed unconcerned by anything except the lack of light by which to walk; they ran and scurried like rats through the shadows, hoping there was nobody waiting around the next corner to steal their money or their lives.

Keph still had the flick-knife in his sleeve. He wondered briefly about holding somebody up and stealing what they had on them – rings, coins, bracelets – but held himself back when he realised that they would then become like him: penniless and homeless. Desperate as he was, his sense of decency overcame his concern for his own troubles, and he continued on his way.

He soon knew when he had reached the southern side of the city: the streets became louder as he came across more inns and gambling houses. He passed a few that he knew, receiving passing remarks from the drunks who had been thrown out after their abominable behaviour. Some asked him for money. Others asked him for a drink. Others asked him for company. He gave none of these, but continued towards the inn he frequented the most regularly, where he hoped he could spend the night at least partially comfortably.

The *Dovetail* was one of the newer additions to the inns in the city. It was more solid than the others, having been built using more recent designs and principles. One main advantage of this was that it became frequented by more and more high-class citizens with money to spend. Any pickpockets aiming to target the wealthy among their clients would be here, as would all the swindlers and sweet-talking conmen, not to mention those women who went to somewhat more ... extreme ... ways of getting money out of the rich men.

It had two floors above its ground floor, not the usual one floor as was common among the older establishments. The paint was thicker and still held something of a shine to it, and the light inside was somehow brighter and warmer, and more homely. The sign above the door showed, unsurprisingly, a dove's tail. The words underneath it read:

Bring unto sorrow a flagon of joy!

If there was one thing Keph disliked about the place, it was its encouragement of depressed people through its doors.

But then, isn't that exactly what he was?

Deel would have loved the poetic irony of it all.

Keph made his way past a snoring heap on the steps up to the inn's entrance, and stepped inside, closing the door behind him. Immediately he squinted and stopped short as the vast number of lamps and sheer size of the blazing hearth in the middle temporarily stunned him. Once accustomed to the dazzling amount of light, he made his way to the bar at the far end of the humid room and took a seat beside a thin old man who was doing more coughing than drinking.

He glanced over his shoulder at the inhabitants of the room, seeing a trio of youngsters in rich clothes carousing in the corner near the door, a bunch of old men talking in low tones around one of the large tables, a pair of outlandish-looking people in heavy cloaks and large hoods with expensive-looking blades at their hips, and a young lady sat at the small table under the stairs. Upon seeing him look over she made eye contact, held it, and raised her eyebrows at him.

The man beside him coughed and spluttered once again, and Keph quickly moved away towards the young lady, eager to be with someone more his own age than an old and clearly ill man. She looked up as he approached.

'Don't bother to ask,' she said. 'Hurry up and sit down, otherwise someone else will make a move on me. Someone older and less likeable.'

Taken aback slightly by her abruptness, Keph dropped his backpack by the table and took a seat opposite her, with his back to the room.

'Am I intruding at all?' he asked. 'I can leave if I am.'

'No, stay,' she said. 'I could use some company.' She looked away briefly, then, catching sight of his backpack, said, 'Where are you off to?'

'I wish I knew,' Keph replied. 'I can go anywhere, and yet nowhere at the same time.'

'Are you a poet? You sound like you're talking in riddles.'

'No, I'm not a poet. But one of my oldest friends is. He's the king's fool.'

'What are you then?' she asked, leaning forwards, fixing her bright green eyes on his. 'What do you do?'

'I used to work in the palace,' he said. 'In the kitchens. I used to cook for the king, and sometimes wait on him myself.'

'Sounds like a lot of fun,' she said. There could have been sarcasm in her statement, but there was also what appeared to be a good deal of genuine interest as well. Before he had time to decide which it was, she continued. 'You say you used to. What happened? Why are you here of all places?'

'The king decided it was time he relieved me of my duties. Let's leave it at that,' he said firmly, suddenly aware of how much he was telling her about himself without knowing anything about her in return.

'Fair enough,' she said. 'I'm Nadia.' She held out a hand. Keph took it in his own, noting how coarse her palm was, but at the same time how soft her grip was.

'I'm Keph,' he replied.

'Good to meet you, Keph,' Nadia said. She was a fraction longer than was usual before releasing his hand, which he retracted with apprehension. Quite why he was apprehensive, he couldn't fathom. But it was there; a feeling in his gut previously unknown to him.

'You too, Nadia,' he said. 'So what do you do?'

'This and that,' she said evasively. 'My work can be a bit . . . rough . . . sometimes. Other times it's quite nice. Depends on who I'm with. I get by, at least.'

'I suppose that's all that matters now,' Keph remarked.

'Yes, I guess it is.' She fell silent. He could feel her watching him closely, even though he avoided her gaze. 'You're very distant,' she observed. 'You have that look in your eye that makes me wonder what you're hiding. You are hiding something, aren't you?'

'Not really hiding,' he replied. Then he hesitated. 'Bad things have happened to me recently, and I've been angry and upset about them at the same time, and it all just came out at once, and I want to forget what I said and did. Two people have been the targets of my anger this evening, and I don't want to make you a third.'

'That's very sweet of you,' she said, 'but people seem to release their anger and . . . frustration . . . on me anyway. Part of the job, I guess.'

That feeling in Keph's gut twisted itself into a knot as he began to comprehend exactly what her job was.

'If you're expecting me to want to . . . you know . . . I can't pay you. I have no money, no trinkets – '

'For a man like you, my services are free.' Again, she locked gazes with him, almost daring him to look away. Then she leaned forwards even further. 'You're much better than the men I usually get of an evening, and I'm more than willing to show you my room.'

'You stay here?'

Nadia was silent. She cocked her head slightly and continued to stare at him. Then she said,

'I have to stay somewhere, and here's as good a place as any.'

'What if I want to refuse your offer?'

'Where are *you* going to stay then? You said yourself you have no money. I'm offering you the use of my room for the night, and if you don't accept someone less desirable will. You wouldn't force me into that would you?'

The knot in Keph's gut twisted again, and the apprehension returned, mixed this time with a significant amount of curiosity. Something about her caught his interest. Something in the way she looked at him. That bright green stare that showed intent and desire and willingness. There was something alluring in those eyes; not beauty, not attraction, but hope.

Hope for her that he would accept, and hope for him that she could help him. Maybe he did need to release something, or maybe he just needed someone different. Someone new. Someone unknown and yet remarkably familiar. Someone who would be willing to know him and take him as he was now, not compared to what he had been.

Someone who could give him hope.

He nodded, somewhat reservedly, and followed her up the stairs.

Chapter 19.

Nadia's room was on the top floor of the inn. Keph followed her up the first flight of stairs, and then again up the second. Though the bar itself was warm and brightly lit, the floors above were significantly darker and colder. Through cracks in open doors Keph caught the sound or sight of a crackling fire in a fireplace, but neither the heat nor the light made it through to the corridor outside.

Few people were outside their rooms, and those who were appeared, for the most part, to be in the bar downstairs. It made the journey upstairs with Nadia all the more awkward: he didn't know what to say, if anything was to be said at all. She appeared similarly reserved, never looking round at him, but continuing to lead him upwards.

The top floor was darker, colder, and quieter than the one below, with thinner corridors, lower ceilings and fewer rooms. Nadia led Keph to the room closest to the top of the stairs, unlocked and opened the door, and stepped back to allow him inside.

There was very little in the room: a decent enough bed, with clean sheets and a stable frame, a small annex with a wash basin, and a window overlooking the city. From it Keph could see the huge silhouette of the palace – the walls and the towers all shapeless hulks of darkness in the night.

Nadia followed him inside and locked the door, then came and stood beside him.

'Missing it already?' she said.

'I've been away from it before,' he replied. 'I've come out here a few times, or to other parts of the city, but I've always known that I would soon be back inside those walls, serving the king and his household. But this time it's different. I'm not going back.'

Slowly, her arm slipped inside his, and he felt her hand on his shoulder.

'I felt the same when I left home,' she said. 'I haven't seen my family for years. I think they're still in the city somewhere.'

'At least you have a family.'

'And you don't?'

'No, I don't. Not anymore.'

He pulled his arm away and stepped back, putting a distance between himself and Nadia.

'But you did. Recently.'

The encouragement in her eyes was all he needed.

He told her everything. From his work with the Segrata to the rebellion, to all the death and the destruction, the king's outburst, Deel's defection. Everything. This young woman who made him feel so different, so new. And she knew everything now, and she listened with intent. She never questioned or challenged him, never prompted him when he faltered, never mocked him for his emotion. Only when he had finished did she speak.

'You're dead on your feet. Sit down before you pass out.'

She herself sat on the bed. It being the only place to sit, so did Keph. But where she made herself comfortable, crossing her legs with her back to the wall, he rested on the edge, wary of committing himself despite her openness.

'Now,' she said, looking him directly in the eye again. 'You have a choice, Keph. Right now this bed looks very appealing, mostly because you're on it. I can see you're not at your best, and I won't force you to if you don't feel up to it . . . but if you're willing to give it a go, so am I. It's not every day a nice young man like you comes in here. Besides, you seem to have something inside you that needs releasing. Why not here and now?'

Keph found he had no answer. Her directness and her allure left him somewhat stunned. She shifted closer, beginning to loosen the ties on her dress.

'You're thinking about it,' she whispered. 'You want it, don't you? You want me.'

Again she moved closer until her legs straddled his body and one hand was on his chest, the other on his cheek and her face only inches from his. She continued to whisper softly to him, her breath warm on his mouth.

'And I want you, more than I've ever wanted anyone. I want you to hold me, to take me, I want you to make me – '

Keph's mind snapped to a decision.

He wrapped his arms around her, pulled her close, and flipped her onto her back, their locked gazes fiery and intense.

Then he stood up and backed away, leaving her sprawled on the bed.

'No,' he said firmly. 'You're the one who wants it. I don't. I don't want to do it just because we're here and we can; there would be no point. I can see your appeal, and I admit I like you, but I do not want someone of your profession taking advantage of my position. There is nothing you can do for me except give me a place to stay for one night without any trouble. Can you give me that, or do I have to leave you to the mercy of someone else?'

Her eyes had never left his, and her expression had never changed. She still regarded with those deep, bright eyes and that tilt of the head that spoke of a mixture of admiration and amusement.

'You're the first person I've met who resisted me,' she said. 'I like that, and I respect that. I guess I've overpowered so many men in my time I don't know how to do anything different to them.' She sighed and smiled grimly, bringing her knees up to her chest. 'I wanted to get out of this, once upon a time. In many ways I guess I still do, but once you're here you're kind of stuck. There's so much I wanted to do with my life, but I won't be able to do any of it. Not now I'm stuck here.' She looked up at him, but now her eyes were merely mirrors of Keph's own melancholy. 'They say the Jade Peaks are beautiful this time of year; rimmed with gold in the autumn sun, backed by a scarlet sky. But that's a long way away, in another life. A life that might have been.

'It's dark here, Keph. It's so dark I can see the light of those other lives I could have had. I can lie here after . . . after I've worked . . . and I cry myself to sleep every night because I know there's places I could be, things I could be doing.'

'Like what?' There was something in her look – something honest and sincere – that made him revise his opinion of her. There was something about her to pity, just as he pitied himself. It made them more alike.

'I wanted a husband, and a family. I wanted to marry a nice, decent man and raise a family with him. That wonderful life so many people have. I wanted it too. I still do. But who would take someone like me? The only men who come through here are so high up the ladder I'm nothing more than a *good time* to them. What I do for a living is no better than what rats do in the gutter. How could anyone take a . . . someone like me away from all this?'

'Perhaps they would feel a measure of compassion for you. After all, you don't enjoy the inferiority of your . . . profession . . . like others would. Perhaps if you could convince them someone you really do hate it, they might help you out of this.'

Nadia raised her eyebrows at him.

'And how would I convince him of that? I don't know fancy words like you do. All I know is . . . how to . . . you know.'

'You've shown me you hate it. You've told me. And I hate to see you doing this.'

This time it was Keph who made the eye contact, and kept it until she looked away.

'So what about you?' she asked, now looking anywhere except at him. 'What do you want to do with your life? Job? Family?'

'I don't know,' he replied. 'I don't even know where I'm going, let alone what I'll do when I get there.'

'That's a shame,' she said. 'Because when I said just now I wanted to marry a nice, decent man . . . well . . . I . . . I wondered if maybe, if things were different . . . if you could afford to . . . would you take me with you? Would you . . . would you be that nice, decent man?'

Keph stayed silent, more than a little surprised at her question. He tried to work out an answer, but she continued before he could.

'I know it's sudden, and I probably shouldn't ask you that, and I don't expect you to say anything – what can you have to say? – but I need to know if . . . if things could have worked out.'

She looked back to him now, but this time it was as though she was expecting a reprimand.

'I know,' he said, 'that if things had been different – if I had the money to support us both – I would be more than willing to take you with me. I don't really like the position I'm in, and you don't like the one you're in. I think we both need someone right now, to get us through. But I can't stay here and you can't come with me.'

'I know. But – '

'But,' he said firmly, 'I will make you a promise, Nadia. I don't want to see someone as pretty and as good-natured as you go down this route; I hate to think what lies at the end. I will leave tomorrow, and I will find some money, and a place to live, and when that's all settled, I will come back for you. I will take you with me, once I know we can afford it. That's the only thing stopping me right now: I can't even support myself, let alone us both. But when I can, I'll be back. And you'll have that nice, decent husband, and you'll have that family. You'll see the Jade Peaks in the autumn. You'll have everything you wanted and more, but I can't do it for you right now.'

He watched his words take effect on her. Slowly, her expression changed as she comprehended what he meant. Her eyes dropped, her lips parted slightly and her mouth began to smile. She looked back up at him.

'What happened to the miserable man I picked up in the bar?' she said. 'The selfish one who didn't care for me a few moments ago.'

'You changed him. We're both as unfortunate as each other. I need someone like you, and you need someone like me. Even I can see the sense in that.'

'You do mean this, don't you?' she said. 'You're not going to just go off and leave me?'

'I would never do that. I've given you my promise, and I'll keep it.'

'Keph,' she said suddenly, as though struck by an alarming thought. 'Keph, why are you doing this? Is it because you just feel sorry for me? Or is it . . . do you . . . do you love me?'

'In truth, I don't know. I don't love you in the romantic sense of the word, but . . . I want you. Just now, we could have . . . and I would have been willing to. But we didn't, because I don't want to be just another man. I want you to mean something, and I want to mean something to you. I want you, and I want you to be happy, but I don't think this could be called love. Not like that.'

Nadia laughed. It was a small, shy laugh, accompanied by an equally small, shy smile.

'You're so sweet,' she said.

'I've been called many things recently,' said Keph. 'But you're the first person to call me sweet.'

'You're also inexperienced.' She grinned. 'I could tell that just by sitting on you. You didn't know what to do with your hands, or the rest of you. I can teach you so much I'll blow your mind.' Then suddenly she regarded him with curiosity. 'Something still bothers me,' she said. 'What does this mean?'

'What?'

'What does all this mean? I want you, you want me, it isn't love, you feel sorry for me even though I do a job we both hate, and we both need each other. It doesn't make sense. What does it mean? You say you don't want to . . . you know . . . unless it means something, but this whole thing doesn't seem to mean anything.'

'It means a lot. It means a change for both of us. But it doesn't mean anything real. It doesn't mean . . . love . . . or anything physical . . . or anything like that. It means an escape for you, and hope for me.'

'I guess.' Nadia looked away. 'So, what now? What are we going to do?'

'I want to rest,' said Keph.

'Can't blame you. I'll let you have the bed. I won't use it tonight.'

'Where are you going?'

'Not sure. I still need to pay for the room, so I might just give out a few small favours. Nothing major.'

'Small favours?'

She stood up and moved towards him.

'Something like this,' she said, and kissed him lightly on the cheek. 'A little something to remember me by, until you come back for me. You will come back, won't you?'

'I've given you my promise already. I'll come back. I just don't know when.'

As if driven by some instinct, he pulled her close and rested his cheek on the top of her head, feeling the surprisingly soft smoothness of her hair on his skin. She leaned her own head on his chest and whispered up to him.

    'Thank you.'

Chapter 20.

Nadia left soon afterwards, intending to spend much of the evening down in the bar to allow Keph to rest. It was now two days since he had slept in a proper bed, and more than that since he had felt fully rested. It felt good to lie on a bed again, even if the mattress was a little thin, and to know that he would be able to rest in peace, undisturbed and uninterrupted.

Nevertheless, he found it hard to sleep. Every time he tried, he was assailed with visions of cruel depravity. Every time he closed his eyes he saw himself as though from outside his own body, and he watched as he tortured and maimed the prisoners at his mercy.

The Segrata interrogation cell was all too familiar to him. It held so many memories, so many experiences he would rather forget. And yet every time he closed his eyes he was there again, watching himself and his brutality as though he was a spectator to his own ruthlessness. He watched himself breaking countless arms, fingers, knees; he watched as that abhorrent sword cut and sliced and thrust into his prisoners. He heard the screams and the snaps. He could smell and taste the sharp iron tang of the blood that spattered the floor and stained the blade and splashed his cloak in crimson.

The cloak. Even though he could see barely anything of the man underneath it, there was no doubt it was him – he felt the impact on his fist as he punched, the crack of bone beneath his boot.

And he hated himself. He had known at the time that his vicious actions were immoral and wrong, and yet he had also believed them to be necessary. Since then he had discovered that he had been deceived, but he had hoped he would never have to see what he had been like before. He knew he had been cruel and brutal, and he knew now it had not been necessary – it had only been wrong. It was as though some supreme power was punishing him for his ignorance and his naivety, his willingness to be deceived.

Every punch he had ever thrown, every kick, every bone he had broken and scar he had opened, every gloat he had ever made was being shown to him over and over and over until he hated himself more than he ever remembered hating anything else. His stomach lurched as he felt as though his soul was being ripped apart.

Only dawn provided respite. With the rising of the sun the visions dissipated, leaving only vague impressions and patchy memories. He felt light inside, lighter than he had felt in a long time. He felt strong and whole, knowing that things could only get better now. Yes, Jerl was dead, but there was nothing that could be done now, and all his memories of his brother were happy and bright.

And he had found a friend in Nadia – an unlikely friend in unlikely circumstances – but a friend nonetheless.

And who knows? Maybe something more, eventually. But only time will tell.

He got up and went to the window. Now that the light of day was above the horizon, the palace was much more distinct than it had been the previous night, its edges sharper and its shape somewhat crisper, and Keph could clearly see now that the place where the west wing usually stood was now occupied by the last whispers of smoke from the bits of wreckage and debris that still smouldered in the courtyard.

It was strange to think that on this side of the palace walls the city was running its daily business, not knowing exactly what was happening behind the gates. The citizens would be sure to have seen the collapse of the west wing from the city itself, but why it collapsed or who had done it they could never guess.

It was a confusion, chaos and naivety that Keph was glad he was getting away from now.

As he put on his shirt, Deel's scroll fell from the pocket and landed lightly on the floor. In the new light of the new day it seemed somewhat less foreboding, more a curious oddity now than a portent of doom. He picked it up and found it no longer felt as heavy as it had done yesterday.

Perhaps it really was worth reading. He moved back and sat on the edge of the bed, before unrolling the scroll and reading its contents.

Well then, Keph. Here we are, parting ways. I had always hoped that when we parted ways it would be in better circumstances than this. By the time you read this I imagine you will be about to leave the city, or maybe you have left already, having come to terms with Jerl's death and the king's actions against you. I don't expect you to want to be reading this; I think it's more out of curiosity that you're reading this than out of respect for what I'm trying to do for you – as I write this you are sitting in my room looking unhappy and, dare I say it, suicidal.

You're not the only one. You're not the only person to have lost a brother today. Every single person who died today had a family somewhere – a father, son, mother, daughter, brother or sister. You are not the only person to have lost someone you love and care about. I have too: Jerl was my friend just as much as he was your brother. But am I responding in the same way as you? No.

Well, perhaps that's because losing a friend is different to losing a brother, and I can understand that. But the point I'm making is that thousands of people will have lost someone they care about today, not just you. Yes, there will be people who feel the same as you, and there will be people who don't, but right now, even though they too have lost someone, they can do nothing about it. They can't avenge their fallen loved one. They can't take up a sword and do what they feel is right. But you can.

You can, Keph, even though I know you don't want to. Right now you seem to want to live the rest of your life in misery and darkness, and I don't want to see you do that. You don't have to live your life that way. Besides, I know I'm going to go over to work with Gadric, but the baron hasn't won yet by any means. The king and his men still have a good defensive position in the north wing, and even though he may not be at his best, he has the anger now that will make him aggressive and hard to contain. He will be willing to fight and to kill to maintain his hold on his kingdom, because he's scared of what will happen without him. And Gadric seems to have lost his grandson. I can't imagine what that must be like, but I doubt the baron's going to let his feelings show; he's not the type of man to do that.
No, the baron will accept his loss, and he will grieve when the time comes, but right now I expect that he is determined to fight for what he believes in. He will be fighting tomorrow not because of his anger at his grandson's death, but because of a burning, fiery desire to do what he believes is the right thing and overthrow the king.

And think about Prince Borden, Keph! Think of what he must be feeling right now! He allowed you to destroy the west wing so that he could save his brother. But in doing so his son has disappeared among the wreckage as a consequence of your actions. If he had stopped you and let Locan die, he would have lost his brother instead of his son. Think about that choice, Keph! It's a worse choice than you had. Think about what it must be like to realise that in that moment you chose between your brother and your son. Borden would never have been able to save both, and he will know that right now, but is he the sort of person who will sit and despair and sound as though he is going to take his own life? No. But you do, and you have nowhere near as big a reason as he does to grieve.

So why are you making this so dramatic? Is it because you're looking for sympathy, or because you want to be guilty for something? Because if you want to be guilty, damn well do something to be guilty about! You have nothing to be guilty of except doing as you were ordered to. Bad things happen, and we can never stop them all, so why are you so intent on this crusade of despair? You can't go back and change what happened, but you can learn to live with it. And whose fault was it that Jerl died? Certainly not yours, because you were doing what you were told to do. You might be the older brother, but you can't always be looking after the younger one. No, it's not your fault, Keph. It's not even Jerl's, because he too was doing what he was ordered to do. Jerl was killed during the rebellion, and the rebellion has been caused by King Cassien's failings. If anyone is to blame for all this, it is the king himself. He is the one who has caused the rebellion, and therefore Jerl's death, and your expulsion from the city.

Now I've said my piece, so it's time for you to make your choice, Keph, because everybody else has made theirs. Are you going to leave in brazen, barefaced cowardice because you're too weak to stand up for what you believe in? Or are you going to avenge your brother, take on the king, and make the world a better place for everyone, including yourself? Look to Borden and Gadric for examples – they are doing what they believe is right, and they will continue to do so until either they too die or they succeed, regardless of their losses. They're not afraid to stand up to the king and avenge their fallen. You should not be afraid either: the king is a tyrant and a monster, and he deserves to be overthrown. This is your chance to make the world a better place for everyone.

Think, Keph. Think very hard. And if I don't see you at the palace when Gadric makes his final attack, I'll know exactly what to think of you. And I'll make sure others think the same. It's for your own good, Keph. Please, trust me on this.

Deel.

As Keph read, he could see that towards the end of the letter his friend's handwriting was becoming less neat than it had been at the start, as though he was channelling all his emotions – his frustration, his belief and his passion – through his pen and into the words he wrote. Keph supposed that ultimately, every poet and playwright did the same. Once they had something to say that they really believed in and felt strongly about, they would write frantically and relentlessly until everything was out on paper for all to see.

And this was no different. Deel had used that genius brain of his to give his words such impact and such power that as much as Keph had wanted to ignore them when he first began to read, he could not help admitting that they had gone straight to his heart.

And, what's more, it was all true. Only now, when reading Deel's words, did Keph see how foolish and how selfish he had been. How weak he had been! It was ridiculous that he had even thought of abandoning the city to fend for itself. And Deel was counting on him being there, otherwise what sort of future would he have in Sorl if he wasn't? Before, he had been too blinded by his service to Cassien to realise the king was a tyrant, and then he had been too blinded by his hate and despair to allow himself to think properly. Only now did he see the only course of action that was at the same time logical, right, and just.

Again he let his gaze stray out of the window to the palace. The day was bright and crisp, the sky was blue, and there was a battle to be won.

He stuffed the letter back into his pocket, grabbed his backpack and ran out of the door, down the stairs and into the bar. In his haste he almost ran over an old man with a wooden leg and crutch. His face was haggard, his hands gnarled, and he wore on his chest a string of insignia denoting a multitude of military honours. He drew himself up like the soldier he clearly used to be and stared Keph in the eye with the sort of stare only an officer could carry off.

'Where are you off to in such a hurry, young man?'

'I'm going to do what's right,' Keph said quickly, without thinking about what he was saying or who he was saying it to. 'I'm going to overthrow the king!'

'Aye, you do that.' The veteran nodded sagely. 'A kingdom needs a shakeup once in a while. Give him my regards, point first and right up to the hilt.'

Keph continued to run, barely comprehending the meaning of the man's words. He rushed out the door and turned onto the road towards the palace. The streets were starting to fill with people now as the shopkeepers opened up and the workmen went off to work. Traders set up their stalls, lining the streets and the market place with their vibrant awnings and outlandish wares, but Keph paid them no attention as he dashed through the gaps in the crowd, drawing cries of surprise from those he ran past and outrage from those he ran into. Someone even called for the City Watch to give chase, but by the time the Watchmen had been called for, Keph was gone. Besides, he didn't care if he drew attention: all he cared about was reaching the palace in time to be of some use to Gadric.

Finally he burst through the last remnants of the crowd on the street to the palace and sprinted for the gates. Two soldiers were on guard, and on closer inspection Keph saw that they bore Baron Gadric's emblem. As with the guards the previous evening, they stood and barred his way.

'Nobody can enter the palace,' they said sternly. 'By order of King Cassien.'

'Not likely,' Keph said. 'You're two of Gadric's men; I know that emblem. Take me to the baron before I lose my patience.'

'Who are you?' they demanded. 'Why do want to see the baron?'

'My name is Keph,' he replied. 'The baron knows me by name, although he may see me as an enemy.'

'Then why seek audience with him?'

'Because I want to help.'

'Help with what? There is nothing going on in the palace that the baron would need your help with.'

'Don't play the fool,' Keph snapped. 'I know about the rebellion and the baron and the king and everything that's been going on. And I'm here to offer the baron my services. So just take me to him, there's a good man.'

Chapter 21.

Baron Gadric, his leg still wounded from the previous day's fighting in the west wing, stood in the centre of the palace courtyard, deep in conversation with Borden, Locan and Jessa, all of whom were already armed and armoured. As Keph approached, Jessa was the first to notice him. The two of them locked gazes, and he saw her hand stray to her belt, where the short sword with which she had killed Fadrinar hung. Gadric saw her gaze shift, and followed it. Upon seeing who it was that was approaching, his brow furrowed and his eyes turned colder and harder. Then he limped past Locan to stand face to face with Keph. He did not address Keph, however, but the guards.

'What the devil are you doing?' he barked. 'Why is this man not restrained? And how did he end up outside the palace?'

'Sire, we didn't know he was dangerous.'

'Dangerous? That's an understatement. This man is a member of the Segrata. He's one of the king's secret police. They're brutal, unaccountable. Why is he not restrained? Have you searched him?'

'No, sire.'

'Well then damn well search him. I wouldn't be surprised if he has a knife on him somewhere.'

Knowing that to refuse would be to put his plea of peace in jeopardy, Keph allowed them to take his backpack and knife, and the letter from Deel. Being just a scrunched up piece of paper though, Gadric had it discarded along with the rest before having Keph forcibly restrained by the two guards.

'Well?' he demanded crisply. 'What have you got to say for yourself, Keph? Coming here in broad daylight with only a knife and some clothes? Surely the king must be going mad if he thinks this is going to work.'

'I'm not acting for the king anymore,' Keph explained. 'I am my own man now.'

'And you expect me to believe that Cassien has so casually rid himself of the Segrata agent that caused my grandson's death?' Gadric shook his head slowly. 'I don't think so. Try again. Try me with something better.'

'Read that piece of paper,' Keph said, indicating Deel's letter with his head. 'If that doesn't convince you of my intentions I don't know what will.'

Borden picked it up and handed it to Gadric, who proceeded to skim the letter quickly. Then he looked up at Keph.

'Deel?' he said. 'You know Deel?'

'We've known each other since we were children,' Keph replied. 'He has arrived hasn't he? He told me last night he was intending to defect.'

'Aye, he made it,' Locan said. 'He's currently working on his play.'

'Well go get him,' snapped Gadric. 'I want him to verify this. And bring something for him to write on – I want to be sure this hasn't been forged at all.'

They waited in silence for a few minutes while Locan fetched Deel. The scrawny little playwright appeared from out of the south wing at an awkward sort of run.

'Keph!' he cried. 'Oh, Keph! You have no idea how glad I am you read my letter. I've been worried sick for you all night. Ever since you left my room yesterday I've been wondering if I'll ever see you again. And yet here you are, and here I am! Together once more, just like old times. And on the correct side this time.'

'Please calm yourself, Deel,' Gadric sighed. 'I want you to write something for me.'

'Anything, sire! Anything at all! A heroic poem, perhaps? A – '

'No,' Gadric said sharply. 'Nothing like that. Just write a few words, would you? I want to compare your handwriting to this letter, just to make sure there is no mistake.'

'Oh, of course. Of course, sire. Right away, pardon the pun!'

Deel proceeded to scribble a few lines of random words onto the page provided, and then held it up for Gadric's examination. The baron looked at it, and then at the letter, squinting slightly as he looked for any margin of difference.

'I'd say it's the same,' he conceded. 'Wouldn't you, Borden?'

'I would, father,' Borden said. 'But I must ask you, Deel: where do you think of these things?'

'What things, sire?'

'*O for a muse of fire, that would ascend the brightest heaven of invention, a kingdom for a stage, princes to act . . .* Where do you think of it? Come to think of it, what does it mean?'

'I what?' said Deel, clearly startled. 'I wrote that? I don't remember writing that! Let me see, sire, let me see! That sounds wonderful!' He bustled round to look over Borden's shoulder, mouthing the words on the page as he read them. 'Good heavens!' he cried. 'I have! Oh, such a stroke of genius if I do say so myself. The beginnings of my next great work! The romance is almost completed, sire, and as soon as it is I shall begin work on this next one.'

'If you really have to,' Locan said. 'But please try to make it a little less soppy than the romance. Something that really excites people. Something more real, perhaps?'

'Yes, I shall indeed!' Deel stuttered. 'I shall. Something dark and serious . . . a king of Sorl with a claim to the throne of Andaria. Nobles who betray him, a beautiful Andarian princess, and a battle! A battle against all odds! A heroic finale, sire. Heroic deeds! And a speech, a rousing speech, iconic even – '

'Take him away now,' Gadric said to the guards. 'I can't stand him anymore. Put him back where he belongs – with his plays, his poems, and his insanity. We have no use for it here.'

Deel allowed himself to be taken away, more concerned with his own ravings than with where he was being taken. Then Gadric turned to Keph.

'Well,' he said. 'I suppose we ought to welcome you to our ranks, Keph. As long as you can promise that you have left the king and the Segrata behind you.'

'It was the king and his Segrata that caused my brother's death,' Keph replied. 'I'll serve Cassien again when hell freezes over.'

'Very well,' said Gadric. 'I hope you understand that after what happened last time you were with us, I'm slightly reluctant to give you a second chance.'

'I do, sire. I'm grateful you've allowed me to serve you properly this time. But there's one thing I want to make clear, baron,' he said firmly. 'When this is all over, I'm taking a purse of money with me and leaving for good.'

'So you're in this for the money as well as the revenge,' said Jessa sternly. 'That's a cruel way to honour your brother.'

'I came back to fight for Jerl's sake,' said Keph. 'But I don't intend to stay afterwards; too many bad memories now. And to get anywhere I'll need money. The treasury is rich enough that it can spare a small purse of silver.'

'It's a fair enough offer,' Borden said. 'You're an honourable man, Keph. I think you deserve it.'

'Well if you think he's honourable enough,' Gadric said, 'you can have him in your retinue again. We'll see about the money afterwards, once everything and everyone is accounted for. Now get him armed. We've got a king to topple.'

Keph was given a sword, shield, helm and a mail shirt, so that he was armed and armoured in the same fashion as the rest of Gadric's men, and placed in Borden's contingent. When he had decided to join Gadric, he had never given any thought as to what sort of role he would have. In retrospect he was never going to have been given any sort of command role, and even being one of the normal soldiers – one of the many who would be doing the same as him – made him feel more a part of the rebellion than anything else could have.

The remaining three hundred of Gadric's men were distributed evenly among the baron and his sons, each of them commanding roughly a hundred men. Jessa placed herself with Locan, knowing that it was with him that she would be the safest: Gadric was injured and Borden was not the best warrior to have as a lady's leader and protector. In among the men of Borden's contingent, Keph found himself stood next to the soldier named Drogan, who had been his guard only a couple of days before.

'Good to know you've got some sense now,' the big soldier said. 'I just hope you can use that sword well enough to survive.'

'I've been trained in the basics,' Keph replied. 'Segrata training. And I have a little experience.'

'Well then let's hope it's enough to see you through,' said Drogan. 'I'd hate for you to die only moments after seeing sense; it would just make everything a bit pointless.'

'I doubt there will be enough resistance to cause any trouble,' said Keph. 'Barely fifty men escaped the west wing yesterday.'

'Should be a walkover then,' Drogan remarked. 'Might not even have to bloody my sword.'

They fell silent, waiting for the order to advance. Keph glanced up at the windows of the north wing, watching for any sign of movement within, but there was nothing. Neither shutter nor curtain moved, and there was no noise coming from inside. No shouted commands or orders, no sharpening of blades, or rushing of feet. It was as though the entire wing was deserted, like an ancient temple covered in the dust and sand of years gone by.

The rebels too were silent, awaiting Gadric's order. The only noises were the shrill whistle of the wind as it swirled inside the high walls of the palace courtyard, and the snap, flap and crack of the pennant atop the north wing. It was the only one left; all the others had been torn down by the rebels, the vast majority of whom now stood in the centre of the courtyard, armed, armoured and ready to fight.

All three hundred of them.

True, it was almost six times what Cassien had left in the palace, and it was a marvel he had not yet surrendered, but once they did take control, it would certainly be hard to hold onto the power. Granted, other nobles in the kingdom would welcome a new king, but there were others who would not. And in the city itself there would be people who were discontent, who would rise up against Gadric's new regime. The real question was not whether they would succeed in taking over the throne, but whether they could keep hold of it once they had.

'Listen up!' Gadric said loudly, snapping Keph back to the present. 'I think it's traditional in times like these that I give you a speech now – something inspirational and heroic. But we're not here to be heroes; we're here to do a dirty, gritty job that nobody else has the courage to do. That in itself is reason enough to fight on one more time and be proud of what you're doing, for the good Sorl and her people. So . . . swords out, shields up, let's go overthrow a king.'

He turned and strode towards the main door to the north wing. Borden, Locan and Jessa led the rest of the army on behind, towards the last refuge of King Cassien. Upon reaching the doors, Gadric stood aside and nodded to Locan, who took his dozen strongest and largest men and began to charge the door down. Being merely large doors and not castle gates they soon split and buckled under the impact of Locan and his men, before crashing inwards in a shower of splinters. In a moment, Locan was leading the charge inside, but stopped short upon meeting no resistance.

'There's nobody here,' he growled. 'They must be elsewhere, the cowards.'

'If I know my uncle,' said Jessa, 'he'll have retreated to his throne room. He wants to protect his throne, so he'll do it literally.'

'Then that's where we're going,' said Gadric. 'Lead on, my lady.'

Jessa led the way at the head of Locan's company. Gadric followed on with his, leaving Borden's company at the back of the advance as a rear guard. Not that anyone actually thought it necessary, but Gadric was in his rights to play safe.

They met no resistance in the corridors, and Borden made a point of having his men search every room they passed as a precaution. But nothing happened, and nobody was seen. No servants, no soldiers . . . nobody. Once again Keph got the feeling the wing was like some sort of long forgotten temple of another people, with a surprise or a trap waiting at its centre.

They reached the throne room in good time, and Jessa stopped outside the doors. At Gadric's command, Locan pushed on them. Finding them unlocked, the large prince stepped through into Cassien's throne room, letting the rest of the army follow him at a rapid pace.

Cassien was indeed there, sat in his throne with his breastplate on, his shield strapped to his arm and his sword naked on his lap. Beside him stood Queen Alsarra, wearing neither armour nor weapons, but instead her deep red robes and silver circlet. Arrayed before the throne's dais knelt not fifty palace guards, but nigh on five hundred strangely-clad figures.

Each one wore a solid iron breastplate, greaves and boots, and a full mask of dark metal, each one moulded in the shape of a human face. Some were clean and smooth, and others roughly bearded. Some were old, and others young. Some were twisted into contortions of rage, fury or sorrow, and yet others were placid and calm, the serenity itself unnerving. Each man was armed with his own choice of weapon – some wore shields and wielded either swords or axes, but others stood holding long spears with barbed tips, or keen, serrated knives, or cruel and wicked looking halberds. But regardless of this, they all wore a small cape about their shoulders, darker than ash and emblazoned with a golden tongue of flame.

The rebels filed into the throne room, with Gadric leading his men to the centre of the open space directly in front of the dais and the mysterious warriors. Locan led his to the right, and Borden took his to the left. Upon seeing the strange warriors more than a few of the men shuffled their feet and cast their eyes about for a route of escape.

'Checkmate,' Cassien grinned, rising slowly from his throne. 'You have lost, baron. You've lost now. It's over. Even with all your traitors.' He shot a glare at Jessa, who stared back coldly, and then to Keph, who met the king's gaze with a blankness which, he hoped, gave away no emotion. 'Even with all your traitors and little tricks,' Cassien continued, 'I have still outwitted you.'

'Give in, Cassien,' Gadric said. 'The more you resist, the more likely we are to kill you instead of arrest you.'

'And even if I do give myself up to you, you'll still kill me anyway,' said Cassien. 'So I might as well make things as hard for you as I can. I'm going to fight this through to the end, Gadric, mark my words.'

'And what about your queen?' demanded Gadric. 'What about Alsarra? Will you be so foolish as to condemn her to a life of despair and misery as a consequence of your own actions?'

'Alsarra is the only person in this world who has any sympathy or understanding for me. Yesterday I was on the verge of taking my own life, and she persuaded me not to. She convinced me there was still a chance, and she was right. I had forgotten about my secret weapons.'

He spread his arms out in front of him, indicating the kneeling warriors.

'You should have signed that trade agreement, Gadric,' he smiled. 'You remember I said that I had managed to get a full cohort of the Dashaar's Dragon Warriors? Well, I forgot to mention that they were already on their way. They arrived last night, via a back door to the palace, and now they stand between you and me. Did you ever wonder what on earth possessed me to go on that hunting trip with you, Borden? And then to have that talk afterwards and make you an offer? Time, baron. I played you for time, and I won. I gave these Dashaar the time they needed to arrive and protect me by playing silly games of etiquette and civility with you. Well I'm afraid that game's up, baron. Lay down your weapons and you'll get a fair trial.'

'A fair trial, perhaps,' Gadric said. 'But the charge will be high treason and the penalty will be death. If I'm going to die, I'm going to do it properly: fighting for something I believe in. And so are my men.'

'So be it,' said Cassien. 'If that's your decision, I think it's about time I killed you all.'

'Think again, Cassien!' shouted a voice from the gantry above. 'Everybody, open up!'

Chapter 22.

From all sides, a volley of crossbow bolts shot through the air, thudding into the Dashaar Dragon Warriors. All bar a few found their mark, and suddenly over a score of the Dashaar were dead.

But the shock of the volley did not last long: in a matter of seconds the Dashaar had wordlessly formed themselves into a close, tight formation with their weapons raised, and were marching rapidly and silently towards the rebels.

'Form up!' cried Gadric. 'Close order!'

The rebels obeyed, moving closer to one another in their contingents, forming, like the Dashaar, a small but compact battle line.

A second volley of bolts swept in from overhead, felling yet more of the Dragon Warriors. A few were aimed towards Cassien, but the king reacted too quickly, bringing his shield up in defence and letting the bolts thump into it. Then he motioned for Alsarra to stay back, before moving forwards to join the Dashaar, clearly hoping to escape the eye of whoever was firing from the gantry by losing himself in the fighting.

The Dashaar moved neither left nor right in their advance, making solely for Gadric's contingent. Locan and Jessa made to move in from the right, and Borden from the left, in a pincer movement, but the Dashaar on the edges of the formation merely turned on the spot and dropped to their knees in a bristling wall of swords, axes, shields and spear tips, halting the princes in their tracks.

Regardless, some of the rebels still tried to rush the Dashaar line in the hopes of overpowering them through brute force, but were dispatched with a casual flourish of their opponents' weapons. The man in front of Keph was one of those who left the line in his overconfidence, or his impetuousness – whichever it was – and Keph suddenly found himself in the front rank of Borden's contingent. The prince stood a few men away to his left, and Drogan appeared suddenly on his right. Ahead, the Dashaar just knelt like cast iron figurines, with their masks in contortions of almost every conceivable emotion.

And the rest of the Dashaar were bearing down on Gadric and his men with implacable inevitability, but to his credit the baron held his ground.

'Brace!' he roared, and raised his shield, before dropping his weight and setting himself to receive the assault. His men, as always, followed his example.

Then came the third volley of bolts from the gantry, slicing into the rear ranks of the Dashaar on the flanks with fearsome accuracy. On his flank, Locan seized the opportunity the sudden attack provided and led his men in a furious charge against the enemy ranks. He swept aside the first man he encountered, before punching deep into the rest, followed closely by Jessa and the rest of his men as they set about trying to dismantle the Dashaar line.

Borden followed his brother's example, leading a slightly less forceful charge, but what it lacked in impact it made up for with clinical precision: Borden's first blow landed squarely in the tiny gap between the Dragon Warrior's breastplate and shoulder guard, causing his opponent to reel backwards and create a gap.

Keph made sure to follow close, singling out as his opponent a Dashaar wielding a large, two-handed sword, in the hope that in such a confined space the huge blade would have little room to swing and he would have an easy kill. But as soon as he stepped into range, the blade clove down towards him and struck the stone floor only inches from his foot, sending sparks flying from the contact. Then in the same fluid movement he brought it up and lunged towards Keph, who only turned it aside with a frantic wave of his shield. The blade skimmed off, and Keph took the opportunity to rush in close and make a slash towards the Dashaar's exposed side. His sword struck home, cutting deep into the Dragon Warrior's flesh and drawing a line of blood. The masked warrior staggered back and dropped his sword, and Keph leaped on him quickly, finishing him with a stab to the neck.

By now Cassien had led the main body of Dragon Warriors into contact with Gadric's contingent, and was making short work of the baron's men. Through a combination of his own brutality and physical power and the inexorable, cold relentlessness of the Dashaar's attacks, the king was leading his warriors closer and closer towards Gadric. The baron may have been a skilled swordsman, but he was still injured from the previous day and his men were beginning to lose their faith as well as their comrades.

Even the fourth crossbow volley did nothing to deter the Dashaar, even though it thinned their numbers yet again. The prize was in sight, and nothing was going to make them stop now.

Even Keph, from where he stood shoulder to shoulder with Drogan, was able to hear the titanic, feral roar that escaped Cassien's lips as he slammed his blade into Gadric's shield, almost splitting it in two with a single blow and sending the baron stumbling backwards into the arms of his men. He righted himself quickly, but clearly the haste and franticness of his retreat had done his leg more damage, and he stood on it weakly, his face set in a tight grimace.

But Cassien did not relent, stepping in close and bringing his sword around in a large arc before sending a huge backhand swing thundering into Gadric's chest, shearing through the mail shirt and rending a huge gash across the baron's ribcage. The force of the blow, combined with the weakness of his leg, sent Gadric tumbling away across the floor to come to rest a few yards away, limp and unmoving.

'Defend the baron!' shouted the remainder of his men. 'Defend the baron!'

But before long they too were cut down without mercy, and Cassien began to advance on Gadric's body.

Keph redoubled his efforts, and finally himself and a few others, including Borden and Drogan, broke through the Dashaar battle line. Leaving a few to mop up the remaining Dragon Warriors, Borden led a rush against the rear of those who had been fighting Gadric and his men. The clamour of the impact caused Cassien to turn. Seeing Borden approach, his lips twisted into a savage grin.

'Like lambs to the slaughter,' he snarled. 'One baron down, two princes to go.'

'Three princes!' shouted the voice from the gantry.

A tall, lean figure swung over the gantry's edge and dropped to the floor, a loaded crossbow in his hands. He fired a bolt straight towards the king, who merely stood and stared incredulously, too stunned to react. But the bolt struck only his arm, piercing the armour but doing very little to impede him.

'Have that, my liege!' Talan cried, discarding the crossbow and bolts and ripping his sword free of its sheath, before rushing across the throne room towards the king.

With a word of command Cassien turned the Dashaar around to face the new threat, but they were barely organised by the time Borden hit them, followed almost immediately by Keph, Drogan and Talan. With the resolve and determination of Borden, physical power of Drogan and swordsmanship of Talan, the Dashaar were easily overpowered. Keph added what he could, but being no soldier it was nowhere near as significant a contribution as the princes and their best warrior.

Soon Talan, Borden, Drogan and Keph were face to face with the king, but from over on Locan's flank came a sudden cry. Jessa had been separated from the rest of the rebels by two Dragon Warriors and was clearly outmatched.

Talan looked over, and then back to his father.

'Go on, lad,' Borden said quickly. 'We can take the king.'

Talan was gone in an instant, dashing to save his lady like one of the heroes of old.

'I'll deal with him later,' Cassien growled. 'En garde, you mongrels!'

Then without warning he lashed out at Borden, who stepped aside and sent his own blow lunging back. Drogan and Keph also struck back, but for such a large man Cassien was surprisingly light on his feet, dancing backwards and swiping again, the length of his arm and of his sword keeping his attackers temporarily at bay.

They were only ever to make a couple of attacks at a time before once again Cassien was able to counter and put some distance between them. He seemed content to wait for them to make a mistake, and then seize upon it in a flash, but Keph was also content to wait: out of the corners of his vision he had seen the crossbows turn their attention to the stragglers of the Dashaar, as well as thinning out those who remained to fight Locan and his men.

And suddenly, before Cassien knew what had happened, he had been forced back onto the dais upon which stood his throne and his queen. Below him, every single Dashaar Dragon Warrior was dead, as were most of Gadric's men, and perhaps even the baron himself. A few of those rebels who were not wounded or exhausted were hurriedly tending to Gadric's wounds as best they could, but there was no telling whether he would live or not.

And arrayed at the bottom of the steps were the only ones who still had the courage to fight him. Keph stood breathing heavily, with an exhausted Drogan at his shoulder. Locan spat a clot of blood and stared at the floor. Talan and Jessa stood hand in hand, their blades raised and ready. Borden grimaced and squared his shoulders.

'It's over, Cassien,' he said. 'You've lost. Your men are dead and you're vastly outnumbered. Don't make us fight anymore; I don't want this whole matter to be resolved through bloodshed.'

'Then you shouldn't have opposed me,' Cassien replied. 'What happens if I kill every single one of your family? What will happen then? Who will lead this kingdom back to the glory and riches to which I have led it?'

'You may have led it to riches,' Locan growled, 'but not to glory.'

'And neither I nor my father have any intention of leading it the way you have,' Borden added. 'You have ruled through terror and brutality and ruthlessness. That is no way to treat your subjects.'

'And if you kill me, how many of my subjects do you think will actually take kindly to your new rule?' said Cassien. 'You have all committed treason in going against me, and anyone with any sense in this kingdom will see that and turn against you. If you kill me, you will be in power only long enough to see what a mess you have made. Then the masses will rebel against you, just like you have rebelled against me, and drag you down into the dirt! And then what state will the kingdom be in?'

'We're not acting alone,' said Talan. 'We'll have the support once we take over: Count Seldin had pledged his support, as have Dukes Darrit and Cardil. And we have the Andarians on our side.'

'Even they will not be enough to save you from the rest of the noble families,' Cassien said. 'The rest of them support me, as do the Dashaar and the Vallusi. Strike me down if you wish, but be prepared to face the consequences.'

'We've always known there would be consequences,' said Borden. 'But that didn't stop us then, and it won't stop us now. Time's up, Cassien. Are you ready to die?'

'Never.'

The king swung his blade in a huge arc, sweeping it in front of him and sending Borden jumping backwards. Talan and Jessa seized the opportunity, lunging towards Cassien's exposed side, but were almost caught by the blade's return swing, and they too had to scramble away.

Even when so vastly outnumbered, Cassien still had a knack of making sure he was facing every direction at the same time, and either his blade or his shield was there to deflect any attack coming his way. Not even the six of them combined could find a way inside his guard, and it soon became apparent that some of them were not only tiring, but verging on exhaustion – Keph and Jessa in particular. Keph soon felt his arms grow heavier as he struck, blocked and parried again and again in an attempt to break through Cassien's guard.

It may have been easier for them if they had all attacked at once, but Borden, being the cagey fighter that he was, and Jessa, having lost most of her energy and fervour, were often drawing back and waiting before closing the distance once again. This gave Cassien the time and space to focus his attacks more, and Keph lost count of the number of times he was almost decapitated or swept aside by one of Cassien's strikes.

They all knew that it couldn't go on for ever. Something had to give soon, on one side or another.

And it did.

In a move bolder than any he had done before, Cassien rushed towards Locan with his shield out before him. The prince's wild blow skimmed off it, leaving him completely open, and Cassien thrust his sword into Locan's side.

As the prince staggered away and slumped against one of the pillars, Drogan stepped in behind Cassien, sword raised for a killing blow. But Cassien was too good, quickly reversing his own blade and stabbing behind him, catching Drogan in the thigh without even looking. The big soldier grunted and toppled as his leg gave way beneath him, but before

Cassien could land a final blow, a single crossbow bolt slammed into his back.

With a cry of rage and pain he whirled round, looking up at the gantry for the person who had shot him.

'My liege!' Jessa shouted, and once again raised Talan's discarded crossbow to her shoulder. Even as Cassien stared in shock at his niece, she fired again, and the second bolt cracked into his chest, punching through his breastplate and into his skin.

Even then, he did not falter. Instead, he began to move towards her with long, determined strides. But before he could reach her, Talan and Borden had stepped in front of him and barred his way. With a guttural growl he pressed forwards, slicing towards Borden, but the prince's shield swung up to meet the blow, catching the king off balance.

Keph, seeing the opportunity to do what he had returned to do, moved in behind Cassien and rammed his sword through his back, before sliding it out swiftly and cutting it across the back of his knees.

The king tumbled to the floor, crashing down onto the stones in a clatter of steel and iron. His shield crumpled underneath him, and his sword spun away, clanging down the steps of the dais, coming to rest amid the carnage in the middle of the room.

Borden stepped up to him and rolled him onto his back with foot, before placing his sword across Cassien's neck.

'Damn you, Gadric!' Cassien snarled. 'Damn you, wherever you are! I'll get you all back for this. One day, when we're all called to account, I will be there to see that you all get what you deserve.'

'Think that if it makes you happy,' Borden said coldly. 'But right now you ought to be thinking of yourself: think about how many people you have had killed unnecessarily, without trial or reason. You have been the one to bring this kingdom to its knees after all the success your father had. When you're called to account on that day, far in the future, how many people will you have to answer to? Hundreds? No. Thousands, Cassien. You will have thousands of innocents to answer to, all of whom were killed ruthlessly and mercilessly by your order. So perhaps instead of swearing vengeance on us all, do yourself a favour and prepare to face all those people. Because like us, they won't be afraid to face you this time around.'

'But they deserved it! Every last one of them! They defied me – betrayed me. There is no forgiveness for that.'

'No, my liege,' Keph said. He stepped close and knelt down next to Cassien's head, glaring hard into the king's bloodshot, weary eyes. 'There is forgiveness to be had in this world, even if you don't want to see it. You have never wanted to see the good in this world. You have been so preoccupied with holding onto the power you feared to lose that you have failed to pay any attention to the needs of your kingdom. And as soon as someone had a problem that they wanted you to help them with, you thought it was a challenge to your authority. That is ignorance, and blindness, and fear. That is your fear talking, Cassien. You have never wanted to help this kingdom, but to keep hold of your power and authority. And the only way you knew how to do that was to leave people to die, or even order their deaths, so that nobody would dare to challenge you.

'Have you ever thought about those who were lower than you? Did you ever consider that they too needed what you needed – food, shelter, and respect? Of course not. Because you were scared of them. You were scared of them because you didn't know them, and you could never take the time to do so.'

'I am still your king!' growled Cassien. 'I am still your king!'

'No, you're not,' said Borden. 'You're not my king: kings have kingdoms.'

Then with a grim finality he drew his sword across Cassien's throat, watching as though transfixed as the blood dripped from the tip of the blade onto the stones of the throne room floor.

'The king is dead,' he said quietly, then looked up towards where Gadric's body lay, tended by three soldiers. 'Long live the king.'

Chapter 23.

The aftermath was almost as bad as the battle itself. Now, in the tranquillity of survival, those few who had made it through could finally see how much death there had been in the space of less than a morning. The sun had not yet reached its peak when the last sword was sheathed and the last helmet removed.

King Cassien's body still lay on the dais, and beside it stood Queen Alsarra. Since the fighting in the throne room had started she had neither spoken nor moved. Now, she stood with her head held level and proud, as she always had done. Not even her husband's death could provoke a single tear from her cold face. But then, she had never really loved him, had she? It had been a marriage of convenience for both their fathers, and she had never argued.

Did she feel liberated too? Did she feel as though she was free now that Cassien was dead?

It was a question to which only she knew the answer.

Then a solitary ringing drew Keph's attention, and he looked up to see Talan drawing a small knife from his belt. The prince stepped towards Alsarra and held the tip of the knife towards her.

'Your husband is dead, my lady,' he said sternly. 'Will you join him?'

'Talan,' snapped Borden. 'That's no way to treat a lady. Especially one who has not fought back.'

'If I had wanted to join him I would have fought by his side,' Alsarra replied calmly. 'I have never wished for his death; nor have I even prayed for it. But it has come all the same, and I will not complain. Though I wish things did not have to be so bloody.'

'So do I,' said Borden. 'But Cassien was reckless and foolish. If this is anyone's fault, it is his and not ours.'

'The change has come for the best,' Locan added. He was sat up now instead of slumped, with a soldier crouching next to him, bandaging the wound on his stomach. 'If we had not done anything, nobody would have.'

'Yes,' Alsarra agreed. 'It is for the best.' She looked down at her husband's body. 'He was a strong man, Prince Borden,' she said. 'He was a strong king, but his fear and his paranoia led to the misuse of his power. He had a good heart, in the beginning. But the man you killed wasn't my husband anymore. He was a monster, and I will not cry over a monster's death. The man I married was dead long before today.'

At Borden's command, Cassien's body was removed from the room and taken away for cremation. There was to be no ceremony or funeral. Just a pyre and a flame, and then ash and dust.

'What will you do with me, Prince Borden?' asked Alsarra. 'Will I be imprisoned? Hanged?'

'It should be my father who decides,' Borden answered. 'But I fear for his health. Until either he is well enough to decide, or I inherit his title, you are free to roam the palace as you please; I have no quarrel with you, my lady.'

She smiled faintly and bowed her head.

'Thank you. It is good to see that there is still some honour in this kingdom. I shall retire to my chambers. Send word to me only when a decision has been made.'

She left the room at a dignified walk, taking care to avoid the bodies strewn across the floor.

'You haven't welcomed me back, father,' Talan said abruptly.

'No, I haven't. Don't think I'm not happy to see you though; there just hasn't been the opportunity.'

Father and son stood and faced one another properly for the first time since before the attack on the west wing the previous day. Borden smiled.

'What happened to you? Why didn't you come back?'

'I lost most of my men when the wing started to come down on top of us, but managed to slip a score of us out a back door. I have to admit that after that I wasn't thinking straight. I didn't consider things like I should have. I never even considered the rest of you. I knew the king had to die, and I had enough men and an opportunity. So I took it, hunkering down in the wreckage until dark and then slipping in here. We killed all he soldiers that survived the explosion and took their weapons. Then we hid in the empty rooms until this morning. We came here and set ourselves around the balcony to wait for your arrival. The rest you know.'

'What about the Dashaar?' said Borden. 'Cassien said they arrived last night.'

'We didn't see them. If we had, we would have let you know. Things nearly didn't work out.'

'They wouldn't have done if not for you. You did the right thing, son. Maybe Jessa really does deserve you. You're not a boy anymore, Talan, and it does me good to know that.'

Borden turned his attention to Keph, who still stood waiting nearby.

'I think that you have earned your right to walk free,' he said. 'I can see no reason to hold your previous allegiances against you.'

'Thank you, sir,' said Keph. 'I am glad to have been of service to this kingdom properly for once.'

'How so?' Talan said quickly. 'You served Sorl before.'

'I served the king,' Keph replied just as quickly. 'I served the king, not the kingdom. If I had been serving the kingdom I would have killed the king long ago.'

'And yet you didn't,' Talan continued. 'Why?'

'Because I was misguided,' Keph snapped. 'I was too close to the king to see what it was that was really happening. That was a luxury you had that I did not. You weren't tied down by an oath you never fully understood.'

'Talan,' Borden said calmly. 'Go and help with the bodies. I want this throne room cleared as soon as possible. Leave no body, blade or blood in this room. Erase this carnage from our kingdom.'

Talan sheathed his blades, eyed his father suspiciously, and stalked off among the piles of the dead and the pools of blood.

'I apologise for my son,' Borden said. 'He has yet to learn that men do what they do for many reasons, and that those reasons change. I fear it will take him a long time before he has the temperament to deal with people like you.'

'People like me?'

'I'm sorry, I didn't mean it that way,' Borden said quickly. 'I meant that Talan sees the world in absolutes: good and evil, traitorous and loyal, living or dead. He knows that you were once an enemy, and he knows well enough that greed and personal power are both strong motivations for switching sides. He will never fully trust you, I fear.'

'He doesn't need to trust me,' Keph said. 'I don't intend to stay now that Cassien is dead and Sorl is liberated. You have your kingdom, and I have my freedom. For that I am grateful.'

Borden smiled. Then he began to laugh.

'You truly are marvellous, Keph,' he remarked. 'You are truly marvellous: when I first came here a few days ago I saw that the king had marked you as special. And I considered it, and then we talked on that hunting trip. And I knew then that for once the king had got something right. There was something uncanny about you that day, something that made me think that you were the one to watch out for. That's why you ended up in my contingent when we had to keep an eye on you; I wanted to watch your movements myself.

'And I was right. I knew you were something special to Cassien. And yet even though he then went on to insult both you and your brother and to banish you, you still had the fortitude and the guts to come back and face him with us. That is marvellous, Keph. That is true courage.'

'You give me more credit than I deserve, sir,' said Keph. 'It was Deel that made me see this was the right thing to do.'

'I don't think we do, actually,' Locan said. Now bandaged and on his feet, he limped painfully over to stand with his brother. 'I noticed something about you as well. I saw it this morning, in the battle just now. You have a presence about you, Keph. That's something not many people have. But you do.'

'I'm sorry,' Keph said. 'I'm afraid I don't understand.'

'I can see you've had basic sword training,' Locan explained. 'But you're by no means proficient. It was not that, however, that brought you to my attention. It was your very presence. You have something about you that speaks of morals, of justice and of righteousness. You have that determination that inspires others. It inspired me today, Keph. You inspired me to fight on when it seemed as though my flank was lost.'

'Exactly what are you proposing?' Keph asked. There was something apprehensive in both their voices that made him uneasy, as though they were about to say something that they would later either regret or rejoice.

'We know you want to leave,' said Borden. 'But would you consider a place in my father's court? As an adviser or something? You're wise enough and perceptive enough to be a good judge of right and wrong, and you're level-headed enough to counteract many of the more rash nobles we have on our side.'

'But –' Keph began.

'And failing that,' added Locan. 'Would you consider a captaincy of some sort in the army? We would have to brush up your swordsmanship and give you proper military training, but you have the presence of mind and the charisma to carry it through. You could be a great leader if you put your mind to it.'

The proposals took Keph by surprise so sharply that it took him a few seconds to realise he was staring open-mouthed at the two princes.

'I . . .' he began. 'But . . .' Again he struggled for words. Finally, he managed, 'But why?'

'Because after everything that's happened here, men like you are in short supply,' replied Borden. 'You could help this kingdom even more if you put your mind to it. You are more than capable of seeing something like this through to its end. You could be so influential in these positions, Keph. You could do so much to help and protect the people in your kingdom.'

'The thing is,' said Keph, 'I don't feel like this actually is my kingdom anymore. I had everything here taken away from me, and I was on my way out. I don't think it would be the same if I came back, especially in such a prominent capacity.'

'It would never be the same,' Locan agreed. 'You're right about that. But it's going to be different for everyone now.'

'More so for me than for them. I've seen what being part of politics can do: it causes disagreements, it makes wars, it causes countless unnecessary deaths. I don't want to be part of that.'

'But if you were with us you could help to stop it,' Borden insisted. 'You could be the one to stop the wars and stop all those people dying.'

'No, I couldn't,' Keph said firmly. 'Nobody could. Not even you, sir. In the end, if someone wants a war, they'll get a war any way they can. It's part of human nature.'

'And you know a lot about human nature?' Locan said doubtfully.

'I do – I have seen the life of a servant, and I have seen the life of a king. I know better than anyone here what it's like on both sides of the coin, and the first and foremost thing in human nature is selfishness. From selfishness comes greed, and paranoia, and fear. That is why Cassien became the man he was: because his fear took hold. That is part of human nature, and nobody can ever stop the course of human nature peacefully. Not me, not you. No one.'

'But –' This time it was Locan who had to be cut off.

'No, sir,' Keph said sternly. 'I cannot accept either offer. My brother was a soldier, and he died. I will not allow myself or anyone else I know to follow in his footsteps. I will have nothing to do with your army. Nor will I enter your politics. I've seen what it does to a man, however much he thinks otherwise, and I will never willingly subject myself to that. Not now, not ever. I will be leaving the city, and I may well leave the kingdom; I haven't decided yet. But will you promise me one thing before I leave? Do you still respect me enough to grant me that?'

Borden could only nod. Locan looked away.

'Promise me that when things settle down here, you will not let that fear go to your heads. Because if it does, and nobody is there to stop it, you will become just as corrupt and as cruel as Cassien and then you will be overthrown and this dirty, bloody, grim cycle will continue, and more people will die, and Sorl will become a kingdom known for its brutality and fear. Do not let Sorl be known for that. Turn Sorl into a kingdom of happiness and safety, where nobody is scared or oppressed, and where the leaders actually lead. Will you promise me that? Will you promise your people that?'

'We will,' Borden said. 'You can be assured of that, Keph. Thank you. Now, I must see to my father. Goodbye, Keph. And good luck.'

Chapter 24.

Baron Gadric died shortly before midday. The slash across his chest was too deep to be healed, and he had already lost a lot of blood before he could be properly tended to by a surgeon. Keph watched from a distance as the news was broken to the baron's family. Borden dropped to his knees beside his father's body. Locan looked up at the ceiling and closed his eyes. Talan turned away and began to pace, head down and fists clenched.

By now the rest of the bodies had been cleared, and Gadric's was the only one remaining in the throne room. He had been left where he had fallen. He had neither moved nor opened his eyes since receiving the fatal blow from Cassien.

He had never lived to see the kingdom liberated.

Borden received the title of Baron immediately, and straight away sent a runner to Alsarra, telling her that she was to leave the city, but could remain in the kingdom. He offered her Bronze Keep, because, in his words,

'I will be living here now. I have no need for Bronze Keep. It is yours and your family's, my lady.'

Gadric's body was removed to Cassien's old quarters until there was enough time for a proper burial. In the reorganising of what soldiers remained alive under Borden's command, Drogan, for his exemplary actions in the fight against Cassien, was given the position of Borden's personal bodyguard. It was a promotion Drogan accepted without hesitation, and he relished every moment of it, even with his injured leg – the surgeons had told him it would never fully recover, but he would be able to walk, run and ride well enough to be a more than competent bodyguard for Borden. It was also announced that Talan and Lady Jessa would be married before the end of the week was out.

The Jessa who returned from cleaning out the rest of the wing was different to the one who had left. During the battle for the throne room and in the minutes immediately afterwards she had still retained much of her noble composure and feminine demeanour. She returned with her soldiers with a sterner face and a bolder gait, holding the crossbow comfortably and now at ease in the armour.

'How many did you find?' Borden asked her upon her return.

'Three dozen,' she replied shortly. 'Most of them servants. They surrendered themselves, so I sent them away to be temporarily imprisoned until everything is under control. But, there was one I had to kill.'

'Why?'

'The king's valet,' she said, 'decided he would rather fight than surrender. He would not see reason, so I was forced to kill him.'

Keph heard the news with shock and surprise.

Nard had decided not to take Keph's advice. He had decided not to join the rebels, and had instead decided it would be better to die in the wrong service than to do the right thing and defect.

'Not everyone can see reason like you can,' said a voice beside him.

He looked round to find Deel standing at his shoulder, a bundle of papers under his arm.

'I even told him to defect,' Keph said. 'I even told him that you were doing the same, and I made sure that he knew it was the right choice. And yet he still didn't listen.'

Deel turned his head and looked back at him, those quick eyes sharp and piercing.

'Nard was a man who valued his service more than his life,' he said. 'He wanted to die in good, loyal service, even if it was for the wrong cause.'

'But he wasn't right to do that.'

'Right?' Deel continued to stare directly at him. 'After all this, do you even know what constitutes right and wrong anymore? You're not even in a position to judge what's right or wrong. I use the term loosely when I say he died for the wrong cause. Cassien felt so betrayed it obscured his vision of right and wrong, and you were so upset at Jerl's death that your vision too was obscured. And Gadric has been haunted by Cassien's call at the battle all those years ago that started this whole thing off. He could not see what was right or wrong either, though I'll admit he had the best judgement of it in my opinion. His cause was right, but many would say his approach was wrong; too bloody and too violent.'

He smiled grimly. 'It's a shame really,' he said. 'And ironic. You, the king, the baron . . . you were all too blind to see everything properly. But me? I've seen it all so clearly. I have understood so much more than anyone else. But I'm just an entertainer, a poet wrapped up in his own little world . . . a fool, even. And yet I understand more than anyone about all this bloodshed.'

'It seems that nowadays blood is the only way things can be settled,' Keph remarked darkly. 'There's not enough blood in this world for all its differences to be settled this way. There has to be some other way.'

'There is,' said Deel. 'It's called talking. And it happens more than you think. You're starting to sound morose again, so don't. Not everything is settled with blood, Keph. Not everything is settled with violence in this world. People do negotiate. People talk and people understand, and in many cases it works. But Cassien was always trying to stop it working so that he could assert his authority and hide his fear.'

'Is that the only reason for what Cassien did?' Keph asked. 'Fear?'

'Fear is a powerful motivation, Keph,' replied Deel. 'Yes, Cassien did what he did out of fear and nothing else, however much we hope there was some other motivation. He was scared that one day his power would be taken away from him, and because of that fear he ruled like a tyrant, and people started to dislike him, and he was overthrown. It's a cruel cycle really: you fear to lose your power, so you clamp down on your people, who rise up and overthrow you and subsequently strip you of the power you so feared to lose.'

'And it can happen to anybody,' Keph added, looking over to Borden.

'It can,' Deel agreed. 'But I think the new baron has enough sense not to emulate the king's actions. Besides, with more noble families on his side than Cassien had, Baron – soon to be King – Borden has no reason to fear losing his power. I think as well that Borden has a quality which Cassien severely lacked.'

'Which is?'

'The ability to use his power to help people, and to make their lives better and more worth living. He can give people the things they need to get themselves out of the gutter and into a warm home, with a bed and a kitchen and a hearth. He can give them what they need to marry and raise and support a family. He can protect them with his relations with the other kingdoms and, failing that, Prince Locan is a superior warrior; in times of crisis it will be the king's brother – his own flesh and blood – who leads the kingdom. And above all he has a son to whom he can pass his kingdom. Prince Talan, though impetuous with youthful vigour now, will soon grow into a well-tempered young man fit to inherit a kingdom.'

'Yes,' Keph said quietly, looking over at Talan and Jessa, who stood apart from the others, deep in conversation. 'I think so too.'

The last of the soldiers left the room, leaving Borden, Locan, Talan, Jessa and Drogan on the dais. Keph and Deel remained further away, out of earshot of the nobles. They stood quietly for a few moments, until Deel said suddenly,

'So what about you? Eh? What are you doing now? Off to somewhere else still, or are you going to stick around and help everything bowl along? I have wonderful new idea to tell you about –'

'I can't stay, Deel,' Keph said quickly, stalling Deel's ravings before they could get going. 'I'm sorry, but I can't. I was a servant under a tyrant, and I had a brother. Now, it's a new king and a new regime, and my brother is dead. It would be wrong of me to stay.'

'Wrong? We're not back to right and wrong are we? Just when I thought we'd gone away from all this serious, dreary, philosophical stuff!'

'I use the term loosely,' Keph said, smiling wryly.

'Of course,' said Deel. 'I should have guessed. So where are you going?'

'The *Dovetail*.'

'That's not exactly far away is it?'

'I have someone to pick up first,' Keph explained. He glanced at Deel out of the corner of his eye. 'A lady – her name's Nadia.'

'Ah, I see,' Deel said, nodding sagely.

'No, you don't, Deel,' Keph said. 'Not this time. I think this is one of the few things you will not understand.'

'You're in love? I understand that perfectly,' Deel blurted out. 'I wrote a damn play about it.' He ruffled the papers under his arm as proof.

'That's where you're wrong,' said Keph. 'I don't think it could ever be called love . . . by either me or her. She has a certain . . . dislikeable profession.' He raised his eyebrows at Deel, who took the hint and nodded once in acknowledgement. Keph continued. 'Yesterday, when the king banished me, after I had talked to you and to Nard, I went to the *Dovetail* and she was there. Unlike you and Nard, she properly understood, because she too was living a life she didn't want to live. She was willing to let me be me. And I pitied her, Deel. So I promised that when I had the money I would take her out of these dark times and take her with me. After that, I don't know.'

'You say you're going to stop by the *Dovetail*,' Deel said, 'but you never said where you were going to get the money from.'

'The treasury,' Keph replied. 'Borden said before the battle that I could take what I needed, but Gadric wasn't so sure. With Gadric dead though, I guess Borden's decision stands.'

'You don't need to go to the treasury,' Deel said, a smile creeping onto his lips. 'Remember Cassien placed a wager about me bringing in a sleeping draught and a spontaneous friar into my romance? Well, I did it! So, during the battle, I crept upstairs and took the hundred crowns from the king's personal purse. It was all there, ready and waiting for me. I know he said it would go towards my production of the play, but I think I can persuade Borden to give me more than a hundred crowns, so the money is yours, Keph. Every last shilling.'

He produced a worm leather purse from his pocket and handed it to Keph, who took it thankfully, the weight pressing down into his palm.

'Thank you so much,' he said.

'No problem,' said Deel. 'I expected you to refuse. I was all prepared to have another rant at you again.'

'No need,' Keph said. 'I think I know a good deal when I see one.'

Deel grinned and looked down at the floor, shaking his head and chuckling.

'That is one of the worst puns I have ever heard, Keph. Actually, it's so bad it's almost good. But seriously, Keph, one hundred crowns will get you and your lady quite a way. You can easily buy a home in Andaria or Rhenar or Meinon, or if you like you can even get passage on a ship elsewhere. Anywhere. Just remember that it won't last forever.'

'Maybe not forever,' said Keph. 'But at least I won't have to worry so much for a while. Thank you, Deel. You're a good friend.'

'I live to serve,' the poet replied. There was something in his expression that Keph had rarely seen before: sympathy and compassion. Even when Deel had been talking to Keph the previous day about Jerl, the king and the baron, there had been no sympathy in his words or his face. Honesty and purpose, yes. But not sympathy.

'Will you continue to serve the king then?' Keph asked. 'Or will you just write plays and poems from now on?'

'I could never just limit myself to plays and poems,' Deel laughed. 'I have to write songs and jokes as well. I must bring mirth and merriment to everyone I can, king and peasant alike! I will be the fool again. In fact, I insist on being a fool.' He stopped suddenly, then said, 'Don't you worry about me. Worry about yourself; what are you going to do once you get to wherever it is you're going? Will you go back to cooking somewhere, or will you find yourself something different? Something exciting?'

'Good question,' said Keph. 'I honestly don't know the answer. I suppose I'll have to see what's around when I get there . . . wherever *there* may be.'

'So are you off immediately?'

'I think so.'

'You won't stay for the coronation and the celebrations? I'll have my play ready by then. You can be one of the first to watch it!'

'I have no doubt that your play will become one of the best ever, so when it starts touring to the other kingdoms, I'll see it then. I don't want to stay here any longer than I have to, Deel. Too many bad memories.'

'What about the good memories?'

'Those too. But I'll be taking them with me.'

'That's the spirit,' Deel grinned, clapping Keph on the shoulder. 'I knew there was some sense in that head of yours somewhere. Can I take the credit for finding it?'

'Not all of it. Nadia's the one who changed me. I would not have had the sense, or even the courage, to read your letter. For once, I think she deserves more thanks than you.'

'Who would have thought someone you found so dislikeable would prove to be your salvation?' Deel marvelled. 'It's a shame though. I do love making people's lives better.'

'Is that why you do what you do? You write to make people's lives better? I thought it was just for their entertainment.'

'You have learned many things over the last few days, Keph,' Deel said. 'But you have yet to learn the ways of the arts. It is the very entertainment that literature and song provides which makes people's lives better . . . Do try to keep up.'

Keph made to leave, but something stopped him, held him back for that fraction of a second.

'What?' said Deel. 'There's something else, isn't there? One more thing you have to ask the wise old fool. What is it?'

'Yesterday, Nard told me I was thinking evil things in evil times. And last night I couldn't sleep. I kept seeing everything I did in the Segrata. All the violence, all the torture. Was I evil, Deel? Was Nard right? Am I evil?'

'You tortured innocent people, Keph. You tortured innocent people and you maimed them and you made them fear their own shadow, but you're not evil. If you were evil you would have a snake for a tongue and fire instead of eyes and have a name like Alshazaar. When something evil hurts people, kills people, it knows what it's doing.'

'But I did know –'

'Not only that, but they know why they're doing it. Even if the reason is because they're a crazed sadist who sees the world in red, has a cosmic ego and bathes in blood, they still know that that's why they're doing it. You didn't know why you were doing what it was you were doing, not truly. You believed you were doing it because it would help keep the kingdom safe – that's what the king and Fadrinar told you. But in truth you were doing it because the king was scared of losing his power. Now, if you had known that that was the real reason behind your actions, would you have continued to do what you did for so long?'

Keph found he didn't even have to think about his answer.

'No. I wouldn't.'

'And that is what proves you're not evil. The fact that you didn't even hesitate to answer me is further proof.'

'Then what am I?'

'Is it not enough that you're not evil?'

'What am I, Deel? You tell me I'm not evil, but I don't exactly feel like I'm good either. Which am I?'

'You're neither, Keph. Good and evil are only extreme forms of humanity. They are the culminations of basic human instincts. Greed, jealousy, spite. They're all mild forms of evil, just like kindness and generosity are mild forms of this so-called good. We humans can never be truly good; there's always something lurking that holds us back: arrogance, violence, a little grudge. If we could be rid of that something, we would all be gods, and then where would that leave the world? And yet there's something else rooted inside us that stops us falling too far; a glimmer of charity, of compassion, a gleam of love. But only the demons of hell are bereft of that.

'So you see, Keph, there is no good or evil on this plane of existence . . . merely humanity. Neither you nor I are good or evil. Nor was the king, or Jerl, or the baron. We're all human. What you feel inside you isn't evil. It isn't good either. What you feel inside you is humanity – it's that sense of being human, it's that tangible sense of merely existing. It's you. What you feel right now is what you truly are. What do you really feel? At the heart of it all? At the centre of all that turmoil there is one thing you feel that tells you what you are. What is it?'

Again, Keph didn't have to think.

'Freedom.'

'Then that's what you are. Not good, not evil. You're free. Free like you've never been before. You can go where you want, do what you please . . . see who you like.'

He drifted into silence, but the pause was only momentary.

'This new life of yours; you have the money to fund it and the freedom to live it. So why are you still here? Why aren't you gone yet?'

Keph had no answer this time.

'Go on, get going. Take your lady and go. Take her to the horizon, and then keep on going. Don't worry about me. I wouldn't.'

Keph didn't need to be told twice, disappearing in a dash. But Deel seemed not to notice, talking more to himself now that Keph was gone.

'No, I wouldn't worry about me. Who would? Who indeed would spare a thought for mad old Deel and his foolish ravings? Foolish, they say? Yes, perhaps a fool. But a fool who sees, and who knows, and who understands things even the wisest of the Gods cannot begin to imagine. My plays, perhaps, will warrant little more than a footnote in the history books, but what do I care for literary immortality? Can there ever be a piece written or a piece performed that knows as well as I the secrets – the very foundations – of the world? Yes, indeed, don't worry about me. A fool I may be, if only in occupation. But foolish? Nay, never foolish. Wise, though: wise beyond the boundaries of mortality. Indeed, there can be no doubt that I am the wisest of fools.' He glanced towards the doorway through which Keph had vanished. 'Spare me not one single thought, Keph. She needs them more than I do now. She is your salvation after all, even if you don't want to call it love. Indeed, she needs you more than anyone else ever has. Even Jerl.'

Chapter 25.

This time, when Keph left the palace, it was with a clearer head and a lighter heart. Not to mention a heavier pocket. He had with him only the clothes on his back, his small woollen cloak, his Segrata flick-knife and the purse of money Deel had taken from Cassien's quarters.

Really, it was nothing. He had no other clothes or tools like a workman or tradesman would. He would be starting completely afresh, with his whole life ahead and a blank slate to work from. It was liberating.

Liberation. Not only had he himself been liberated by Deel's letter and subsequent return to fight the king, but the entire kingdom had been liberated by the actions of the rebels. And perhaps even by Keph himself; after all, Keph was the one who had dealt the blow to Cassien that caused him to fall to the floor. True, Borden had been the one to make the final strike, but it had been Keph who had given him the opportunity.

'Afternoon, young man,' said a voice beside him. 'Gave the king my regards, did you?'

It was the crippled veteran Keph had almost run over in the *Dovetail* that morning.

'Point first and right up to the hilt?' the veteran continued.

'Not me,' Keph replied. 'But someone else. The man who will soon be crowned king.'

'Ah. Been a proper rebellion has there?'

'There has.'

'Lots of bloodshed and death?'

'Aye.'

'Hmm. Anyone in the king's service still left alive?'

'Just the queen,' said Keph. 'Everyone else is dead.'

'Good gods,' the veteran breathed, shaking his head wearily. 'Is all that bloodshed really worth it? Tell me, young man. Tell me it was all worth something. Don't say the new king will be as bad as the old one. Please tell me all this blood means something!'

'It means everything,' Keph replied. 'I know there has been a lot of blood spilled. Some of it has been my own brother's. But be assured it has all been worth something. The new king will be a better man than the last. Much better.'

The veteran visibly relaxed.

'It does me good to hear that,' he said. 'I'm glad this kingdom will finally become somewhere worth living. If only it had happened earlier, eh? We could all have had better lives.'

'Wouldn't that have been good?' Keph agreed. 'The world seems to be built on *if only* . . . '

Even as he spoke, he trailed off, thinking immediately of Jerl, and how long it had taken before he had stopped saying to himself *If only I had turned back to help him*.

But there was nothing to be done now. And there never could be again.

'You alright, lad?' the veteran asked, peering into Keph's face. 'You look a bit peaky.' But from his expression, it seemed he was able to guess something of what Keph was thinking.

'Just thinking,' Keph said. 'I'm just glad it's all over.'

'I'll bet you are; a nice young man like you getting involved in fighting and killing. It's not right, I tell you. Just not right. It's the old men like me who start wars, so we ought to fight in them, not let the young ones do it for us. Sending you young bloods off to hell while we stay safe in our beds. It's a tragedy, this world. A true tragedy.'

'Aye,' Keph agreed. 'That it is. I feel like I've been through hell, the last few days.'

'Through hell?' The veteran glared at him. 'What do you know about hell, boy? You've not been there yet, not by a long way. You don't know what hell is until you've stood in the middle of a bloody battlefield with thousands of corpses all around you, with the cries of the dying ringing in your ears, with half your damn leg laying a few yards down the hillside. You've seen death, boy, and you've seen blood and corpses. But you've not been through hell yet. I've been there more times than I care to count and look at what's left of me.'

As he spoke, the man's eyes turned harder and his jaw hardened, as though struggling with something inside him.

'Look at what's left of me. I've been through hell, I've seen it up close, and I've lost too many good friends in it. You're too young, boy, too young. You don't know what hell is.'

He continued to glare for a moment, then looked away sharply and grunted.

'Sorry lad,' he said. 'I've seen too much of it for my liking, and left a lot of good men there. They're the ones who know what hell is, not people like you. I feel I owe them this much, some sort of defence of their memories. Personal thing. Officer thing. Means something to me. But,' he said, holding up a finger, 'there's always hope while someone's left to do the hoping, eh? One of my father's phrases. And I like to think I'm the one doing all that hoping, because I can't exactly do much else with my time, and because most people nowadays don't bother.'

'No they don't,' said Keph. 'Nor did I yesterday.'

'What changed?'

'I met a woman who understood what I was going through, and who needs me as much as I need her, and a friend of mine gave me the kick I needed to get back into this world and do something good and right.'

'Heh!' the veteran laughed. 'What are friends for if not to give you the kick? Anyways, your life ain't going to wait for you, so I'll let you get back to it. Stay safe though, right? Good men like you are hard to come by.'

'I will,' said Keph. 'Thank you.'

'Anytime.' The veteran was about to continue on his way, but stopped short. 'By the way, lad . . . I'm sorry about your brother. I'm sure he was every bit as good as you.'

'He was,' said Keph, nodding slowly. 'In many ways he was probably better than me.'

'In that case,' the veteran smiled, 'wherever he is right now, he should have nothing to fear. Remember, lad: it's always sunny above the clouds.'

Then he turned and limped away, his wooden leg clunking on the cobbles as he disappeared into the crowd.

The news of a rebellion in the palace came quickly to the population of the city. Messengers under Borden's banner were dispatched into the streets to announce the death of King Cassien and the imminent coronation of Baron Borden as king.

'King Cassien is dead! His rule has been overthrown by the forces of Bronze Keep, now led by Baron Borden. By right of inheritance, the kingdom passes to the king's niece and ward, the Lady Jessa, who has renounced her claim to the baron and his family, thereby granting Baron Borden the kingship of Sorl. The Lady Jessa is instead engaged to the baron's son, Prince Talan. Both the coronation and the wedding will take place tomorrow morning at the palace. The king is dead – long live the king!'

In the bar at the *Dovetail*, the news was received with mixed responses.

'About bloody time! We need a king who actually helps us.'

'To usurp the throne is treason! This cannot be allowed to continue!'

'Never liked the king. Or his laws.'

'Give us our king back! He knew how to protect his people!'

The irony of this last statement was not lost on the young lady who sat in the corner listening and smiling.

The customers were oblivious to everything around them in their shouted attempts to get their opinions heard; in amongst the chaos that had broken out following the messenger's announcement, a young man entered the bar and made his way to the young lady at the table.

She looked up at him with surprise, and asked him a question. He replied quietly, and pulled a heavy purse from his pocket, dropping it in front of her. Her eyes widened, and she laughed and stared at the purse. Again, she asked a question, but he just shook his head and grinned. He pocketed the purse and held out his hand to her. She took it in her own and hugged him close, eyes brimming with tears. Then they broke apart and he began to talk, to explain. She listened and smiled and cried. He explained that they could go anywhere they wanted and do anything they liked. He explained that they were free now, liberated from what had been, to both of them, times of servitude and isolation.

Then, after a pause, she said two words.

'Thank you.'

And he replied with six.

'Don't thank me. Thank the king.'

Printed in Great Britain
by Amazon.co.uk, Ltd.,
Marston Gate.